Hunted

Bree Coleman

This book is dedicated to my babies. Not just because you all are awesome. You give me a sense of purpose. I'm a stronger person because of you. You make me courageous to the point that I feel like I can accomplish anything. I couldn't have asked for a better team than this one. I love you.

Bree Coleman

Chapter 1

Today was hot, hotter than it usually is in mid-October. It was my first day of my new career as a Project Manager at Sawyer Engineering Inc. I wore a beige, satin blouse, and a leather cognac colored pencil skirt with a pair of nude Christian Louboutin stilettos. For my accessories, I wore a pearl necklace and earring set that I had gotten from Tiffany's a few years ago. I wore a pearl bracelet from Tiffany's as well. My Saint Laurent clutch bag was also beige to coordinate with my blouse. When I left home, I had a fresh blowout, but it'd gotten a little frizzy during my walk from the employee garage to the building.

As I walked into the building the security guard at the front desk stopped me to ask if I needed help. With a smile I assured her that I remembered the directions to my new office on the 8th floor. She said, "Wonderful. Enjoy your day." I told her to enjoy her day as well. I continued to head for the elevators which were already crowded. Usually, I didn't mind taking the stairs, but with these heels on I couldn't wait to get to my desk and take them off. It's a good thing I was early because I ended up waiting at least ten minutes before I was able to catch an elevator.

When I stepped off the elevator it was like a breath of fresh air. All my hard work had finally paid off and it was a joy to finally see the fruits of my labor. There was a bouquet of rust-colored roses sitting on my desk when I arrived. The scent of the roses created a calming ambiance in my office. I inhaled the wonderful aroma of the roses. My day was starting off just right and I was ready to conquer any project thrown my way.

"Ahhhh, that feels so good." I said to myself as I slid my stilettos off underneath my desk. I'd finally sat down and started to check my emails when Erica, the floor's floating assistant walked into my office. "Good morning. Happy first day Ms. Scott. I hope you loved the roses I picked out for you. Mr. Webb said that you loved roses. I didn't want to be too cliché and pick red roses. Besides red roses don't seem to live that long in my opinion." She winked at me and walked out just as quickly as she walked in.

After trying to check my email I ended up having to call the IT Department. They told me that they were going to look at my PC remotely in the next hour or so. I knew that I was going to be out in the field before then so I just asked if they could wait until I returned. Matt agreed to get it done and we ended the call. I decided to do a short walk through to speak to my new colleagues and formally introduce myself. By the end of my tour, I'd concluded that Stephanie, the office manager, was as dumb as a box of rocks.

It took me a little over an hour to get to the construction site that I was assigned to monitor. Traffic was hectic as hell. People were driving like they had nowhere to go and no time limit to get there. It was just far too hot to be sitting in slow moving traffic. When I arrived on the site, I changed into my steel toe boots, grabbed my hard hat and the rest of my PPE before getting out of the car. I had to get an update on the baseline from the Superintendent over the site. The hard hat did no justice for my hair because the wind still blew my already frizzy hair everywhere and the dust only made it worse. I wanted to get this meeting over with as quickly as possible and head back to my cozy office.

"Can I help you pretty lady?" One of the contractors asked as I walked towards them. I noticed he was using a jackhammer, nonetheless, there weren't any ground markings stating what area needed to be excavated. I put on a fake smile and said, "I'm here to meet with your boss's boss. Where can I find him to have you fired?" He seemed to have lost his ability to speak. "No worries, I'll find him." I turned to the other contractors, "Do not touch another piece of machinery without marking your utility locations properly." I watched as they scrambled to do as they were told.

Chuck was coming out of his portable office as I was walking up the stairs. "Good morning, Chuck. How's your day going so far?" I asked.

"I can't complain. How about yourself?" Chuck sarcastically responded.

"Well, it was going pretty good until I caught a contractor trying to work without wearing the proper PPE. Were you aware that your guys were using machinery without drawing any utility markings? Where the hell is your Foreman?" I ask as I look around. "These guys are his responsibility, right? This is unethical. Do you know the amount of trouble we'd be in had someone else seen it? How much money we'd all lose? I wanted my trip here to be smooth sailing but apparently your guys are out here pussyfooting on our dollar, which explains why your triple constraint isn't accurate. Your Gantt Chart clearly illustrated that this project would be completed in three weeks."

"I'll get with the Foreman about the guys being unprepared and I'll have him put emphasis on wearing the proper PPE in the next safety meeting," Chuck says as he rubs his temples in frustration.

"Look, I want that guy removed from the site ASAP because he's a liability. If he gets injured on the job site without the proper PPE on, that's a lawsuit. That will be both of our asses and I don't want my ass handed to me on a silver platter."

"Ok, I'll let Keith know." He said with a strong sigh. "You're a tough one Ms. Scott but I kinda like you already. You know your shit."

"Thanks for the compliment. I have to know my shit so I can be taken seriously. With that being said, when do you expect this project to be finished?"

"There was some damage to the drainage line which caused a larger portion of the street to be excavated. We were waiting on a change order to get approved so we can fix the drainage line."

"Ok, once it's approved, when do you expect to have the project completed?"

"Should be completed within the next two weeks." Chuck said.

"I will approve your EOT for two weeks. Just two weeks Chuck."

Keith, the foreman comes from what looks to be a Porta Potty and walks past the handwashing station. Chuck and I both frown our faces in disgust. I had been at the site for at least twenty minutes already. Keith had to be in there doing one of two things. I'll leave that to your imagination.

"Morning Ms. Scott. What brings you by? Keith asks.

"I've gotten a few complaints about you all missing the project deadline that you were given. Now that you've gotten rid of your load, maybe now you can be a bit more productive." I said as I began to walk towards my car. I turned back and said, "I want that guy gone TODAY Chuck." Then, I heard Keith cussing from a distance.

Back at the office I typed up my report to be given to the director. Chuck stated that the project would be completed in the next two weeks. Although I thought that he was feeding me a crock pot of shit, I still included the EOT in my report. The progress report I expect to receive from the engineering tech this coming Friday will be the judge of that. The client was becoming more impatient. Not only are the contractors a month behind schedule, but this is a $100,000 project that the clients need to have complete sooner rather than later.

Chapter 2

I had been home maybe an hour before my bestie, Kris called me. She moved out here to Dallas about three months ago for a new job as a psychiatrist. I let her talk me into applying for jobs in Dallas and I was blessed to actually get one, a well-paid job at that. That's how I ended up here in Dallas. Prior to the move I had been expressing to Kris how much I needed to get away from our hometown of New Orleans. She told me that there were great career opportunities in Dallas. I jumped right at the idea and sent my resume to a handful of companies. I received an offer from Sawyer Engineering Inc about two weeks later. I met with Dave Fontain the next week for an interview. He expressed to me how intrigued he was with my resume and my ambition. Mr. Fontain wanted me to start shadowing that day.

Anyway, the girls wanted to go out to celebrate my new job. I had only known them for a short while, but we had grown into a little family. We went on a mini getaway two weekends ago to celebrate my new job, but the girls liked celebrating everything. Macey's morning after pill was effective, we celebrated. Angela made it through the workday without spilling her drink on her desk, we celebrated. To my girls every accomplishment was cause for a celebration. That's one of the things I loved about them, never a dull moment.

Kris planned to meet Angie and I at the restaurant. Angela was going to come to my house and ride with me since we lived close to each other, and Melanie and Macey were going to ride together as well. I had already taken my shower and was drying off when Angela came into the bathroom fussing about a spot on her dress.

"Amora, please tell me that you can get this stain out of my dress before we leave. I tried to grab a quick bite to eat before I went for drinks."

"Angie, you know you could've just eaten at the restaurant. I'm in the damn bathroom. I'm going to start carrying you on my taxes because you act like my child." I say jokingly.

"Whatever." She says rolling her eyes playfully. "Please get this stain out before Mel sees it. She's going to talk about how clumsy I am. I don't feel like hearing it tonight. I already had my ass handed to me on a platter at work today."

Trying hard not to let her see my crooked smile I ask, "For what?!"

"Evidently, Paul's disgusting ass had been complaining about the number of laptops I've damaged by wasting liquids on them. Amy called me into her office this morning telling me about eating and drinking at my desk." She changes her voice and starts to quote Amy. 'It not only causes pests, but it also causes damage to our equipment. It's been brought to my attention that you have not damaged just one laptop but two. You're causing the company to lose money. If this happens again you will reimburse the company for every piece of equipment you've damaged and will be terminated. The choice is all yours.'" She switches back to her normal voice. "I wanted to smack her lips off her face. You should've seen her snobby ass."

"She's right though Angie. You can't keep damaging the company's property and think they'll keep you on their payroll. You know I love you but I'm not going to tell you what you want to hear. Put yourself in their shoes. You've said plenty of times that you don't care, and they have the money to replace it. Now they're threatening to take their money back and FIRE YOU. Come on sis, it's not worth losing your job over."

"You know I hate it when you're right. That's why I had to grab a jelly donut. I needed some comfort food." She says then makes a sad face. We both chuckled.

" Just look in my closet for a dress. I should have something in there that you could fit." I say before walking out of the bathroom. I go into the kitchen to pour us a glass of wine. Angela needed to take the edge off before going out. Melanie didn't really care for Angie, so she seldom bit her tongue when talking to Angie. Mel spared no feelings. Mel only tolerated Angie because she was my friend. Angela was a bit of a klutz, though.

Angela walks in fifteen minutes later wearing a red one shoulder dress. She looked stunning. I can tell that she knew it as well. The dress fit her perfectly. We made eye contact and immediately I noticed that she'd been crying. I say, "Girl, come have this drink and leave that conversation behind you. You look good Friend. Angie grabs her glass from the counter and tells Alexa to play "Survivor" by Destiny's Child. I take a sip from my glass then sit it back on the counter. As I walk past Angie, I rub her back and say, "You'll be fine. I'm going to get dressed."

When I get back to my room, I slide into my dress. I was wearing a black jersey V-neck dress. I complimented the dress with a pair of Dolce & Gabbana Ankle-Strap Stiletto Heels, my pearl necklace and earring set, and a black Saint Laurent clutch. My hair was still wrapped from when I took my shower, so I combed it down. I did a glance over of myself in my floor length mirror before exiting my bedroom.

"Okay!" Angela yells as I walk into the living room. "If you weren't trying to catch a man, you're definitely going to catch one tonight honey."

"I'm just trying to keep up with you." I said with a chuckle. "You ready?"

"I sure am. I'm hungry and I done drank this wine." She says while looking at her empty glass. "I need to eat me something before I get sick."

I grabbed my keys from the key holder, and we headed out. The ride to the restaurant was a little under twenty minutes. Angie was the DJ the entire way to the restaurant. She mostly played R&B, but she had a nice playlist going, this could probably be a hustle if she was serious about it. As I backed into my parking spot, I spotted Kris sitting in her car. She was using the rearview mirror to fix her hair and put on lip gloss, which made me remember I hadn't put any lip gloss on myself. After I park the car, I put on some gloss and get out of the car.

"You really think I look pretty?" Angie asks as we make it to the front of the car.

"Yes. Why you ask?"

"You know how Mel is Amora. She doesn't like me." We begin to walk towards the restaurant. "It's not that I care really, I just don't want to give her anything to talk about."

"Just relax Ang, it'll be fine. If you get uncomfortable just signal me and we'll leave. I'm sure Kris wouldn't mind if we left early."

"No way, Mo. Tonight's about you. I wouldn't want you to leave your celebration. I appreciate you." She says as she playfully bumps me.

"Alright now. You better stop before you fall over. You know your ass is clumsy." I jokingly told her.

Chapter 3

We met up with Kris at the door of the restaurant. She's dressed like she's ready to catch a man herself. She was wearing a black halter Midi-Dress. Sis had her back out tonight. She too had on a pair of ankle-strap stiletto heels. You know what they say, 'Great minds think alike.'

"Hey Krissy Pooh," I say as I hug my bestie. "I saw you when we pulled up. Were you waiting long."

"Not really. I've probably been here ten minutes. Had to do another once over." She looks around. "Did you hear from Mel or Macey yet?"

"Nope. I was going to ask you the same thing. I don't want to go in without them, but I'm hungry and our reservation is for 8pm. Mel is always late, though."

"Maybe we should wait a little longer," Angela says. I saw that her comment struck Kris's nerve.

"Angela, you need to stand up for yourself and stop letting people bully you. Melanie is a grown woman just like you.

She knew what time the reservation was for. Hell, she's the one that brought up the idea."

"We can wait another five minutes." I say to Angie to bring her a sense of comfort. Mel's car came through the parking lot as we were getting ready to walk into the restaurant. I knew it was Mel by how fast she was driving. After Melanie parks, she and Macey join us at the restaurant's entrance. We all walked into the restaurant. The place wasn't too crowded. The atmosphere was impeccable. The hostess welcomed us to the restaurant before Kris told her that she had a reservation for five. The hostess then suggested that we follow her to our table. After learning where we'd be seated, I politely asked to be shown to the ladies' room. Angie and Kris followed suit.

In the ladies' room we did our business, washed our hands, and checked ourselves in the mirror. Afterwards, we had a quick pow wow. I reminded Angie to signal me if she began to feel uncomfortable. Kris let us know that she had already intended to leave early because she had to wake up early for work the next day. I checked my hair and dress one more time in the mirror before I exited the ladies' room.

We made it back to the table just in time to order our drinks. I ordered a bottle of Perry's Reserve Rose'. The girls were all looking through their menu. It was all our first time at this restaurant. I knew that I wanted a steak but couldn't decide on which type. "Are any of you ordering a steak?" I ask everyone at the table.

"I was going to order the 8oz Filet Mignon" says Angela.

"That sounds good," I say while looking through the menu again. "I think I'm going to get the double-cut lamb chops with steamed broccoli and crab cakes."

"Ohh, that sounds good." says Mel and Macey in unison.

"Mel, you just get anything but chicken. We don't need you running to the ladies' room to puke." I say jokingly.

Mel laughs and says, "I wouldn't even do you that Mo. I kinda just wanted to get something small so I can drink."

The waitress comes to take our food orders and hurries away. "She must not be used to seeing so many well-dressed, black women sitting at one table." Says Macey. "Baby girl looked like she was uncomfortable the entire time she was taking our orders."

"Speaking of well-dressed." Mel says, looking at me. "Well, aren't you looking like a six-figure salary sitting over there all quiet." Everyone laughs at her joke. "Pun definitely intended," she adds. "How did your first day treat you?"

I sigh. "I had to go put my foot in a guy's ass this morning. Their project is overdue for completion and our client is on the company's ass because of it. Which means they're going to be on my ass."

"Did the contractors say what was taking them so long?" Mel asks.

"He claimed that they had to excavate part of the street to fix the water line. I'm assuming somebody fucked with something they had no business. Can you believe that when I got there, the guys weren't even wearing the proper PPE? They didn't even have the proper markings on the ground. A shit show"

"What?!" Mel yells a bit louder than she wanted to. She looks around to see if she brought any attention to us.

"You heard correctly. The superintendent said that they'd be done in two weeks. Yay me." I say sarcastically. "Tomorrow, I'll be reading the progress notes on another big project. I guess they're trying to make me prove how I earned my spot without sleeping up."

Macey chimes in, "Don't you hate that? They just dismiss all the education and experience you have just because of the way you look. So what, you're young, black, and beautiful. You earned your spot. You've worked hard to get it, now you have to work ten times harder to keep it."

"She's right, Amora." Says Kris. "Look at Mel, she's a female PI. She was the laughingstock when she first stated she was changing her career. The minute these uppity bastards started getting hacked left and right, who did they call? Sure, as hell not ghostbusters. They called this young, educated, black woman for the job."

Angela was quietly sipping her glass of wine until... "Angie, why you so quiet? How was your day at work?" Mel asks with a mischievous smirk on her face.

"It was pretty good actually. Thanks for asking."

"Do you have any issues at your workplace?" Mel was poking. We all knew that Angie was a klutz because she's admitted it many times. Angie was the Administrative Coordinator at a rehabilitation center. She seemed to have loved her job minus the clumsy mishaps that she's been having recently.

"Yea, I have issues just like you guys. People make fun of what they don't know. Simply too ignorant to learn the facts or truth." Angela says and stuns the whole table. "For example, you all know that I'm a klutz because I've said it multiple times. There are some people that I work with that will ridicule and scorn me for what they don't know."

"Go on." says Mel. She was all ears and so were the rest of us. Angela very seldom spoke up for herself and especially to Mel. It was almost like she was intimidated by her.

"Ten months ago, I had a stroke. The doctors didn't know what caused it. It still causes me problems from time to time. Sometimes I lose grip in my hands. Sometimes I may lose my ability to walk or see. Truth be told, I'm not clumsy at all. It's just my way of coping with this transition. It's a pain in my ass but I must live with it for the rest of my life. When you guys make fun of me, I know it's really from a place of love, but I can't say that it doesn't sting a bit. However, I know that my colleagues couldn't care one way or another about my disabilities."

The conversation had gotten a little too deep and emotional so when the waitress came to the table with our food, we happily accepted our plates. No one said anything else about Angie's story. I had already known but to hear her tell the rest of the girls showed her strength. Amy really did a number on Angela when she threatened that she'd have her terminated. It's too bad she wasn't here to hear Angie's story. I could tell that Melanie's heart had softened a little as well. My celebration night was one of the best I'd ever had. Just me and my girls. My new little family away from family.

Chapter 4

I was coming out of the ladies' room when this guy runs into me, almost knocking me over. His reflexes were pretty good because he caught me before I hit the floor. "I'm so sorry, Beautiful. I had my head in this phone trying to send an email to my colleagues." He felt the need to explain himself. I didn't need the explanation, but I appreciated it.

"It's okay." I say as we make eye contact. His eyes were beautiful. They looked to be a chestnut color, and his lashes were long. His complexion was caramel, and his skin looked as smooth as silk. He stood at about six-foot two over my five-foot four frame. He smelled like my favorite scent of Jimmy Choo men's cologne, Jimmy Choo Blue. It had me intoxicated. I was frozen to the point where I could no longer move. He reached his hand towards me for a shake. "My name's Noel, Noel Brown."

"Amora, Amora Scott." We shake hands.

"Love." He says with a smile.

"What do you mean?" I ask with a confused expression on my face.

"Your name means love."

"Yes, it does. How'd you know?"

"Honestly, a few years ago my ex and I thought we were pregnant. She was so excited that she had started looking up baby names and their meanings. Amora just kinda stuck with me. I think it suits you, though. Love is beautiful and you too are beautiful."

"Don't make me blush but thank you." I say blushingly.

"I love your accent. You're not from around here, are you?"

"No, I was born and raised in New Orleans. I just recently moved to Dallas for work."

"Amora what's taking you so- Angela stops in her tracks once she sees me with Noel. "Well, it looks like you're in good hands. I'll be at the car."

"Oh, I'm sorry, I don't want you to keep your friend waiting." Noel says as he reaches into his suit pocket. "Here's my card, I'd love to take you out sometime."

"And she'd love to let you." Angie says as she takes the business card. We all laugh and go our separate ways.

****

It was Friday, October 27th, and it was Noel and I's first date. He wanted to take me to Perry's Steakhouse & Grille. His reason was because he wanted to take me back to the place he'd met me. I had only been that one time, so I didn't mind trying it out again. Noel wanted me to meet him at the restaurant at 8pm, which left me with only an hour to get dressed after work. I wrapped my hair and jumped in the shower.

I was wearing a red sleeveless bandage cocktail dress by Hervé Léger. Since it was our first date I didn't want to reveal too much, got to leave something for the imagination. I was complementing the dress with a pair of platinum ice platform sandals by Jimmy Choo. For the finishing touches I chose to put a pair of Jimmy Choo chain drop earrings and a Jimmie Choo chain necklace with the outfit. I brushed my hair into a high ponytail. I very seldom wore makeup but tonight I wore eyeliner and mascara to make my eyes pop. I was ready in less than forty-five minutes. I did an outfit check and headed to the restaurant.

Noel was at the entrance when I arrived at the restaurant. I glanced at the clock on my dash, it was 7:48pm. We were both early for our first date. Being fashionably late wasn't my thing. It was inconsiderate in my opinion. I parked, checked myself in the mirror once more then, out of the car I went. There was a breeze in the night air, but it was perfect.

"Good evening my lady." Noel says as he kisses my cheek. "I was expecting you to be a little late."

"That's so cliché. I like to be prompt for all my engagements." I say with a smile.

"Good evening. How many?" The hostess says as we enter the restaurant.

Noel speaks up. "We have a reservation for two under Noel."

"Yes, Sir. Right this way."

We follow the hostess to our table, and I notice that it's a little more private than the table the girls and I had. "This is nice. Intimate even."

"I was trying to get us a little privacy so that we could hear each other speak. It tends to get a little crowded on the weekends."

"Oh okay, so you come here often?" I asked out of curiosity.

"No, not at all. I asked questions when I called to make the reservation. I asked the hostess if she could suggest a special seat for a first date." He shrugs. "So, here we are."

"You were prepared. I like that."

"I forgot to tell you how stunning you look tonight. I'm intrigued to see that you complemented me. I had no idea what you were going to wear so I said, 'what the hell, black goes with everything right?'" He chuckles.

"You look handsome yourself. If I didn't know any better, I'd think you were going through my closet." I said with a chuckle. The waitress comes over and Noel requests that she brings us the best bottle of wine they had and a couple glasses of water. She leaves us to do what she was asked.

"So, what convinced you to come out with me tonight?"

"Your persistence. The single rose on Tuesday. The dozen roses on Wednesday. The chocolate covered strawberries on Thursday." I smile. "I had almost a week's worth of reasons to take you up on your offer." Noel smiles and I notice that he has one of the prettiest smiles I've ever seen.

"It's good to know that my gifts made you smile." The waitress comes back to take our orders. I ordered a filet mignon medium well with steamed broccoli and Noel ordered the same. "How was your day at work?"

"It was long." I say with a sigh.

"How so?"

Looking at Noel confused I ask, "You're really interested in how my day was?"

He chuckles. "Of course, why wouldn't I be."

"Well, as you know, I'm a project manager. Today I had to actually manage." I chuckled. "At the moment we have a client that has requested some contractors fix a waterline in a residential community. I took a trip to the site Monday because they were behind schedule. The superintendent told me himself that the project would be completed in the next two weeks. This was Monday. So, today I received a report stating they'll need another week. Their excuse was because they're short staffed. You can only imagine how pissed our client was to find out they must wait yet another week."

"Sounds pretty tedious."

"That's the perfect word to describe it." I take a sip of my wine. "I'll probably need another bottle." We both laugh.

"I must say, you don't find too many women willing to do what you do. What made you decide to go into construction?" Noel asks me.

"My dad was a carpenter until he died."

"Oh, I'm sorry to hear that."

I shrug. "I felt like he was taken away too soon so I decided to follow in his footsteps. I just took it a step further. I love what I do though. Enough about me, what's your story?"

"I was born and raised in Houston. I used to play sports in high school but when I didn't get a scholarship, I decided to go to college for business. I earned my master's degree in business. Now I have a business development company with my brothers here in Dallas."

"When you say develop, are you speaking in terms of helping businesses become better, larger?"

"Not exactly. My brothers and I buy smaller companies that are struggling to keep their businesses running."

"Oh, like the guy on the movie "*Pretty Woman*", I love that movie by the way."

"Something like that."

"Do you love what you do?

"I do. It has its ups and downs, but I do."

"What happened with the pregnancy scare you were telling me about?"

"My high school sweetheart and I thought that we were going to be together forever until we weren't. We were having problems before she found out she was pregnant but once the possibility came of me being a dad, I was excited. I was going to be there for my child whether we worked out our problems or not. She took that as me trying to make things work with her. When we found out that she had an ectopic pregnancy, we were devastated. I left maybe a month or two after that."

I finish off the wine in my glass and pour myself some more, at the same time the waitress brings our food. "Would you all like another bottle of wine or anything else to drink?" She asks. Noel looks to me for an answer.

"No, we're fine with our water, thanks."

"Okay. Let me know if you change your mind." She says as she leaves to serve her other customers.

"I don't have much of an appetite anymore. I just want to listen to you talk." I stated.

"Well, you eat, I'll continue. You're probably wondering why I left. I left mostly to protect my mental health. Our problems were ruining my career. I was trying to get my company off the ground, and she didn't trust me. When I had to meet with different business owners, she was accusing me of cheating. All I was trying to do was provide for her and give her the finer things. I wanted to do nice things for my parents. Some nights we'd argue, and I'd be too tired to hold my meetings the next morning. I loss a few clients because of her and her insecurities." I stop eating with a questioning expression on my face. Noel notices. "No, Amora, I never cheated on her. I left and ended up here. I've been living single in Dallas for the past three years."

"Well, it sounds like you did what you needed to do." I assured him.

Chapter 5

Bumping into Amora Monday night was the most wonderful part of my day. Not only is she sexy, but she's also beautiful. I'll never forget the way she looked in that black dress. The way it accentuated her breast and hips. Her creamy milk chocolate skin. Her intoxicating scent. The glisten in her eyes when she smiled. Her perfectly round ass that I'd gotten a glimpse of when she walked away with her friend. Everything about her was perfect.

Amora called me for the first time the very next morning. My caller ID stated she was calling from Sawyer Engineering Inc. I didn't want to seem like a stalker, so later that day I had my courier bring a single rose and card to her office. He was instructed to leave it at the front desk with security. Of course, I didn't want to scare her away, but I also didn't want to let her get away.

The following Wednesday, I tried to get her to have lunch with me, but she was too busy. Something about meeting with a client for a new project they had just signed a contract for. Amora worked her ass off and I loved it. She had beauty and brains. I had to make her mine. She complemented me in more ways than one. We were both ambitious and career driven. She liked nice things, but she didn't come off materialistic or as a snob. That was something else I liked about her. I had already sent a single rose so this time I took it up a notch. I had my courier deliver a dozen light pink roses. She had expressed to me the night before that she didn't care for red roses although she appreciated the gesture. I took note of that.

Amora called me later Wednesday evening, but I was having a dinner meeting and missed the call. I excused myself to the restroom to send her a text apologizing for missing her call and assured her that I'd return her call after the meeting was over. Before giving her a chance to respond I put my phone into the pocket of my sports coat and headed back to my seat. Upon arrival the guys were taking shots. My big brother handed me a shot, "Take a shot with us lil bro we just closed a deal with Morris Inc. Noble had them sign the contract right after you left the table."

"Awesome!" I said before taking my shot.

"What ya'll feel like doing? Let's hit up a club, get a section, and pop some bottles." Nathan suggests.

"Nah, I think I'm going to call it a night. I'll catch up with you guys later." I say, trying to let my brothers down easily.

"You must be trying to go celebrate with the chick Noble told me about. I know I would. Noble told me you said she was fine as hell." I shot Noble a look and he noticed.

"Yea Nathan, I think I'mma head on home too. I promised Tia that I wouldn't be out all night." Noble chimes in to get Nathan off my back.

"Cool but we're definitely doing something at the crib this weekend." Nathan said, still determined to get us to celebrate.

"Most definitely." Noble and I say in unison. We all stand to leave.

"Great job fellas." Nathans says as he extends his right hand for the rest of us to shake. "I love ya'll." That's when I knew that Nathan must've had more than just that one shot. He always got emotional when he had too much to drink.

"Please tell me ya'll rode here together?" I asked Noble damn near pleading for him to say yes.

"Yea, I drove." Noble said putting my mind at ease. I headed home.

I called Amora soon as I got into my car. She answered on the first ring. "Hey, you." I could tell she was smiling through the phone.

"Hello Beautiful. How was your day?"

A strong sigh came before she said, "it was long."

"I have time."

"I spent most of my day writing project reports and having meetings. One of the new clients we are under contract with wants a project done in two weeks. It took me hours to convince him that the time period was unrealistic. I had to go as far as showing him how long it took for some of the materials to come in. Shot him a few worst-case scenarios. Some of these people with money act like a bunch of self-entitled pricks."

"Tell me about it."

"How was your day?"

"Tonight, my brothers and I signed a contract with a new company. Their company now belongs to Brown Enterprises."

"Congratulations!" She says excited enough for the both of us. "Why aren't you out celebrating?"

"The only celebrating I want to do is with you. Since I ran into you, I can't stop thinking about you."

"Same here. I tell you what, we can celebrate this Friday if you don't have any prior engagements."

"How about we just enjoy our first date on Friday, and you come to celebrate with me and my brothers on Saturday?"

"That sounds like a plan."

"Now that that's squared away, what kind of panties are you wearing?"

"WHAT?!"

I laugh so hard it hurts a little. "I'm kidding Amora. Don't bite my head off."

"Noel, I almost told you something." She says in between chuckles. "You got jokes."

"Seriously though, I can't wait to see you again. You were like a breath of fresh air."

"That's sweet. I'm looking forward to seeing you as well. Where are you on your way to?"

My mind started thinking a million thoughts. Oh, this is it, she's about to invite me over. "I'm heading home. Why what's up?"

"It's just a little past my bedtime. I can stay up if you want me to."

"Get you some rest Love. I just wanted to hear your voice before I called it a night. Good night my love."

"Good night, Noel Brown."

****

Sitting in this restaurant with Amora sitting across from me made me feel like the luckiest man on earth. The woman was beautiful both inside and out. Each time that I've seen her, she's been well dressed. I wondered if she was in the fashion industry until she told me she was a project manager. This woman could put some of these celebrity women to shame with her class and beauty.

For our date night I knew that I had to dress appropriately to take her out. I had to match her elegance with my own elegance. I wore a black two-button suit by Giorgio Armani along with a black button-down shirt underneath. I also wore a pair of black dress socks and a pair of black leather loafers by Prada. To add a little color to my outfit I wore a red tie. My David Donahue cufflinks were onyx and sterling silver.

"Can I ask you a question?" I was curious to know why this perfect woman was single.

"Sure. What's on your mind?"

"Why are you single?"

She chuckles. "Well, my last boyfriend and I were in two different stages of our lives. He wanted to settle down and have kids and I wanted to focus on my career." She starts to play with her food as if she'd taken a trip down memory lane.

"Do you want kids?"

"Of course, I do. I just didn't want any then. I want to be set; I want to own my own home first. I want to be able to be home when my kid needed me to be. And most of all, I didn't want to raise my kids in New Orleans. He didn't want to move anywhere else so…" She shrugs. "I had to do what was best for me."

"Did you love him? Do you still love him?"

She shifts her body in her seat. "Yes, I loved him. Yes, I still love him but I'm not in love with him if that's going to be your next question." We both laughed a little. When we make eye contact, I make a questioning expression.

"After we broke up, he ended up getting another woman pregnant."

"Oh, I'm sorry to hear that."

"It's been years ago. I've moved on. I've grown to love me more. I know my value and I will not settle or do something because someone expects me to."

"I'll toast to that." We toast then, Amora tells me to ask for the check. I do as I'm told. I hand the waitress my credit card and she disappear. She returns about 5 minutes later. I add our server's $30 tip to our total and sign the receipt.

We collect our things and head for the parking lot. I walked Amora to her car which happened to be a Daytona Gray Pearl Audi A5 Sportback S line 45. I chuckled.

"What's funny?" Amora asks.

"I have the same car but mine is black on black."

I reach to open her door for her, before getting in, she turns to me. She kisses my cheek and says, "follow me."

Chapter 6

Once we made it to my condo, I poured Noel and I a glass of Storm Chardonnay Vrede 2017. You could taste a bit of citrus and oak. It also had a hint of pear and vanilla. I needed something delicate like me. Something that would've extended our romantic evening.

"This is a nice place you have here." Noel said as he entered the kitchen after his small tour.

"When I said make yourself at home, I didn't expect you to really do it." I said with a chuckle.

"I gotta be aware of my surroundings. It's not every day a beautiful woman takes you to her home on the first date." Noel says jokingly but I sensed the truth in the joke. He takes off his suit jacket and lays it on the back of my bar stool. I handed Noel his glass of wine and led him to the sofa where we take a seat. I tell Alexa to play some R&B. Noel says, "You do know you can sit closer to me, right?" I move closer.

"Is this close enough?"

"Yes, it is." He says as he wraps his arms around me. "You smell amazing."

"So, do you."

"I call it my 'come get me.' It's Jimmy Choo Man Blue."

"I knew it," I say a little louder than I expected to. "I love that fragrance."

"Do you now?" Noel teases. "What is it that you're wearing?"

"I Want Choo Forever also by Jimmy Choo."

"Great minds think alike." Noel looks at me with seriousness in his eyes. "I wish I could have you forever." He gently lifts my head by my chin and kisses me on my lips. I was mesmerized. I closed my eyes and let my lips part ways, giving him the okay to add tongue. He did and he kissed me so passionately. I felt a tingle shoot down my spine. I became moist in between my thighs. I was so lost in Noel's kiss that I didn't notice him picking up. I backed away from him.

"I like you, Noel."

He lifts me off of the floor and I wrap my legs around his waist. "I like you too and I'm about to show you just how much. Will you let me?"

"Yes." I say as I nod.

Noel carries me to my bedroom. Once we make it into my room he puts me back on my feet. Then turns me so that my back is facing him. He kisses my neck softly as he trails his hands down my back to my perfectly rounded ass and gently squeezes. He slowly unzips my dress as he lands kisses on my shoulders and back. My dress falls to the floor revealing my bare back and black laced panties.

I turn around to face Noel allowing him to see my plump breasts. My nipples were already hard, and my yoni was throbbing. Noel kissed me again, only this time there was more passion in the kiss. He was trying to devour me, and I loved every minute of it. I unbuttoned his shirt while he undid his belt and pants. Moans grew and so did the anticipation. I wanted to feel him inside of me.

Noel finally slides my panties off, putting my fresh bikini waxed pussy on display. He picks me up and I wrap my legs back around his waist. My arms were wrapped around his neck. He lays me onto the bed and begins to kiss my breast. As he makes his way to my nipples, he sucks them alternating from one to the other. My moans grew as my body started to twitch when Noel inserted his finger into my already wet pussy. Then another. He kisses my thighs before bringing his head to my heavenly opening.

His tongue felt warm when it met my clitoris. I swarm. Noel licks and sucks. Sucks and licks. He massages my pearl with his fingers and makes me cum. I cum so hard it was like electricity had shot from my body.

"Please." I begged.

"I want you to come for me one more time." Noel says as he continues licking my clit and using his fingers to enhance my orgasm. I came so hard the second time it felt as if I was lying in a water puddle. Noel stands up and looks at me as I lay in place feeling vulnerable. "You're so beautiful Amora."

"So are you." I say with the little bit of voice I had left.

Noel pulls the covers back. I take the hint and crawl under the covers. He walks around to the other side of the bed and climbs in. Noel wraps me in his right arm as he uses his left hand to massage my clit. "I was letting you catch your breath."

He says with a chuckle. Noel shifts in the bed, and I notice him putting on a condom. He was prepared. *"Why was he prepared. Oh God, I'm so happy I wasn't the only one."* I thought to myself.

When he's done, Noel climbs on top of me. He grabs the back of my head with his hand and kisses me hard. That's when I feel his erection spread my pussy open. He was so long and wide, but his dick fit perfectly inside of my pussy as if it had been molded just for him. I moaned and cried out.

"Yes baby. That's it. That's my spot." I moaned.

"You feel exactly the way I imagined you would. You're perfect." Noel kisses me.

"It feels so good. I don't want you to stop."

He slows his grinds and strokes then he lifts my legs and plunges into me.

"Oh shit." I moan loudly.

Noel lets my legs go and wraps his arms around me. He whispers, "I want you to come for me one more time." I do just that. My body starts to convulse, and my orgasm erupts all over his dick.

"Oh fuck." Noel says as he speeds up his rhythm. "I'm about to cum."

Before I knew it, I was cummin again too. Noel collapses onto the bed next to me, wraps me in his arms, and kisses me on top of my head. We were quiet for a moment then I had to ask the question. "Will you still like me tomorrow."

"Absolutely! After that, you're not getting rid of me." Noel says with a chuckle.

I shift so that I can look at Noel's face. "Can you stay the night?"

"I was planning on it. Amora, I was serious. I'm not going anywhere. You're mine from now on."

"What about tomorrow?"

"What about it?" He says as he softly rubs my head.

"What should I wear?"

"You can wear whatever you want to wear. We'll most likely be in the yard early in the day. Once the sunset Nathan would probably light the fire pit."

"I'm assuming Nathan's your brother."

"Safe assumption. Nathan is the oldest. Then it's me, Norman, and Noble."

"No girls?"

"Nope, my mom and dad had all boys."

"I want a pair. One girl and one boy."

"I can make that happen." Noel says and we both laugh.

I playful hit him. "Shut up, nasty."

"I don't mean right at this moment. I'm talking about down the line."

We drift off to sleep.

Chapter 7

The next morning, I woke up still lying next to Amora. The woman was beautiful even in her sleep. She was sleeping so peacefully, but I had to have her. I was intoxicated by her. Her smile, her beauty, her intellect, her entire being. This woman had me falling hard whether quickly, but I couldn't let her know it. She was definitely wife material, and I was going to make her my wife.

I slide out of the bed and go into the kitchen. I wash my hands and check the refrigerator to see what Amora had that I could cook. She had some eggs and a half gallon of milk. There was a pack of turkey bacon in the freezer, I took that out to thaw. Then, I quietly checked the cabinets for spices and other ingredients. Once I had everything I needed, I made a batch of pancakes.

Amora came strolling in the kitchen just as I was getting ready to scramble the eggs. "Good morning sleepy head." I say with the biggest grin on my face. She made me feel alive. I can't put my finger on it, but she drove me wild. "Morning." She says back a little dry. She stands on her tiptoes and pokes her lips out. I kiss her. Her soft lips sent shock waves through my body.

Soon as I finished frying the eggs I turn off all the burners. Amora was still next to me wearing nothing but a robe. I pick her up and sit her on the island as I kiss her passionately. I need her to know what she does to me. I lose myself whenever she's close to me. I untie her robe and watch as it falls open exposing her captivating body. I pulled a condom out of my back pocket and put it on.

Amora's pussy was so wet that I slid right in. It was mine and I knew it. She wrapped her arms around my head pulling my head to her neck. I kiss and lick her from her neck to her shoulders. I hold on to Amora's hips and I grind harder. She moans my name and begs me not to stop. I had no intentions on cummin any time soon. I could feel her pussy pulsating on my dick, squeezing me tighter. It was too soon. I couldn't let her cum just yet.

I took her down from the island top and carried her over to the sofa where I made her bend over. Seeing her ass tooted in the air made me lose control. I plunge. I grind. I smack her ass. Amora's moans got louder and louder.

"Oh Noel. That's my spot babe. Oh my God you're about to make me cum.

"What you waiting for? Cum on this dick. This your dick." I say as I grab her ponytail and pump harder with each thrust. I felt her coming. It was like a waterfall crashing down on my dick. I felt my legs getting weak. I was about to cum.

"Babe, I'm cumin. I'm cummin. Oh, Noel you...ohhhh babe." Amora screams and I nut right then and there.

I smack Amora on her ass. "Let's eat." I say as I dispose of my used rubber in the trash can.

"It's about time because you just drained what little energy I had left." She says jokingly while walking back to the kitchen.

I wash my hands before grabbing the plates. "Do you want milk or orange juice with your breakfast?" Amora asks.

"OJ."

"My kind of man." She chuckles as she gets two glasses from the cupboard. She washes her hands then wash both glasses. I use the soapy dish towel to wipe off the island that

we'd just made love on. The flashback makes me smile to myself.
I dry off the island with a few paper towels when I'm done.
Amora grabs her plate and has a seat. I do the same. We eat
peacefully.

****

After Amora got dressed, I took her over to my place
so I could do the same. Nathan called me earlier asking if I
minded if he invited a few people. I told him that it didn't matter
to me one way or the other. I suggested Amora to invite her
friends. I knew from the moment he said we would do something
at his house that it wasn't going to be anything small. Nathan
always over did it. He was the flashy brother, but he could hold
his own.

My house was a four-bedroom brick and stone single-
story, single-family home. It had an open floor plan, and it was
spacious. I'd turned one of the bedrooms into my home office
which left my room and two guest rooms for visitors. There
were three full baths, a two-car garage and a very large
backyard. The house was built only a few years before I
bought it. I purchased it because I was planning to have kids in

the future. I needed to be prepared. I didn't want my woman to worry about anything. I had it all covered.

Amora had fallen asleep during the ride; it was about an hour ride from her condo. She woke up when she felt the car stop. "These houses are beautiful." She says looking around.

"You want one?" I ask with all seriousness in my voice.

"Hell yea. This is the reason I work the way I do."

I get out of the car and walk over to the passenger side to open the door for Amora. "And I work so my woman doesn't have to work at all." I say with a smile.

A shy smile comes across Amora's lips. My dick jumps. She was so beautiful. Her skin was radiant. As she stepped out of the car she asked, "You live here?"

"Yes, I do."

"This is gorgeous Noel."

"Thank you. So are you, my lady." I lead the way to the door. I unlock the door and allow Amora to walk in ahead of me. "Make yourself at home." She takes her shoes off at the door. A habit of hers I assumed because she did the same at her home. Once I walked in, I did the same. I loved how peculiar she was about certain things. I was going to make Amora mine. She gives herself a tour of the house and comes back with the look of excitement plastered on her face.

"Oh my God! You have a California King Sized Bed."

"I do." I laugh because she's short. "I needed something that would accommodate my height."

"It'll accommodate more than your height." Amora says with a flirtatious smile on her face.

"Is that right?" I say as I pick her up and carry her to my bathroom. "We'll take a shower together."

"Ouuu. That sounds even more fun." She says then she kisses me. I lean against the wall when I feel my legs getting weaker. The things this woman did to me. My dick grew harder by the second. I put Amora down and turn the water on so it could get warm while we undressed. Amora stepped into the standing shower first, then I soon followed. The water was the perfect temperature, but Amora made it steamy. I backed her into the wall of the shower and begin to kiss her. I rub my dick against Aroma's sweet spot, so she'd feel how hard she makes me.

"You feel what you do to me?" I say as I nibble on her earlobe. "Only you could do this to me." I whisper.

"I hope so." She says in a soft, sexy voice.

I pick her up and just as I'm about to slide my dick in she stops me. "Get a rubber Babe." She tells me. I do as I'm told and hurry back to my love.

"Where did we leave off?" I say as I kiss her and pick her up again. She moans as I slide my dick into her warm, wet and tight pussy. She moans into my ear, telling me how good it feels. I bounce her on my dick until my arms get tired. She pleads for me not to stop. I put her on her feet and bend her over. I grind slowly as I watch the water run down her back into her hair. "This is my pussy." I say as I smack her on her ass.

"Yes, baby. Yes."

"I can't hear you." I say as I dig my dick further into her pussy. With each plunge you could hear our bodies slapping against each other.

"Yes, Noel. This pussy is yours, babe." She moans. "I want you to kiss me." I turn Amora around so we could kiss. She stands on her tiptoes as she holds the back of my head forcing my tongue to go deeper into her mouth. I was falling for this woman. I needed her. I wanted her. I pick her up and pin against the shower wall. I interlock our hands above her head while I pumped and grinded. Her moans grew louder. I nibble on and kiss her neck gently. I can feel myself about to explode. I let Amora's hands go. She holds on to me tightly. She's about to cum too.

"Oh my God! Shit! Noel, baby, I'm cummin. Babe, I'm cummin." She moans and screams. I become undone. I kiss her as I put her feet back onto the shower floor. She hugs me and I grab her ass. "You're perfect." She says with a smile. We kiss. I step out of the shower to flush my rubber and get back in to wash. After we're done in the shower we get dressed.

Chapter 8

We pulled up to Nathan's house around three o' clock in the evening. His house was just as beautiful as Noel's home. There was smoke coming from the yard along with a sensational aroma. My mouth began to water. I waited for Kris and Angela to catch up with us while Noel was getting the bags out of the car. He just had to stop and get more beer and liquor as if his brother wasn't going to have enough. It was a celebration, right? I asked him to get a couple bottles of wine as well.

"You look like you're still in high school." Angie says smiling from ear to ear. "You look so pretty."

"Thank you. You look good yourself. I see you came prepared to snatch you up a man." I say jokingly.

"Hey Krissy Pooh." I say to my bestie as I hug her and kiss her cheek. "Ya'll did not come to play today. Both of ya'll are making me feel overdressed." I say as we all laugh.

I was wearing a navy, Polo Ralph Lauren cropped cardigan and a pair of skinny jeans by Good American. I had on a pair of tan Cole Haan booties and to match my booties, I had a Little Birdy Wallet Crossbody by Shinola. The only items I had in it were my phone, keys and credit cards. I also wore a pair of large gold hoops from With Love, Jacq. All while Kris and Angie both wore dresses with heels. *"Maybe I should have dressed up as well,"* I thought to myself." It was too late for an outfit change though.

"How you ladies doing?" Noel asked.

"How you doing?" Kris and Angie say back in unison.

I reach to help Noel with the bags. "What are you doing?"

"I'm trying to help you with the bags."

"Woman, I can carry these bags." Noel says with a chuckle. "I just need you to open the door for me." We all head toward the house and I open the door. Noel gestures for us to go in first. I stop in the foyer to let Noel get in front of us.

As we make it to the living room, I see that there's a good bit of people at the so called "little get together." This had to be Noel's entire family. The girls and I speak as we follow Noel to the backyard. He heads straight for the coolers. I help him with the drinks and beer while he breaks the ice to pour into the coolers.

When he's done, he takes my hand and brings me to an older couple. The woman had to be about 5 foot 5 and the man she was standing next to was identical to Noel. *"Oh my God, it's his mom and dad."* I thought to myself. This man was introducing me to his parents.

"Mom. Dad. This is Amora. Amora this is my mom, Betty and my dad, Nathan."

"How do you do?" His mom says as she pulls me in for a hug and kisses my cheek. "You're gorgeous."

"Thank you. I'm doing well."

"Nice to meet you sweetheart." His dad says as he reaches to shake my hand."

"It's an honor to meet you both." I turn to Kris and Angie. "This is my sister Kristine and my good friend Angela. Meet Noel's parents, Mrs. Betty and Mr. Nathan." They all shake hands.

"Babe, I have to introduce you to my brothers." Noel says with his arm around my waist and turns me in a different direction. We head over to the grill where we find Norman. He introduces us then brings me to meet his brother Nathan. "Noble is always late. His girlfriend is kinda loud, so you'll know when they get here."

"Stop it!" I say trying hard not to laugh.

"I'm serious." Noel says. He shows the girls and I where we could sit as he goes to mingle with other guests.

"Mo, that man is FINE!" Angie says.

"Ain't he though? He does have two single brothers." I say mischievously.

The girls and I were chatting it up while I was skimming the room to get familiar with my surroundings. I notice Mrs. Betty looking in my direction and I begin to feel a little nervous. "Amora baby you're the shit. His mom will love you just as Noel does." I think to myself to gain some sense of comfort. I immediately turn to look away. Angela must've followed my eyes because she whispered, "Why is that old hag looking like she wants to kill you with her eyes?"

"Just don't make eye contact with her. I don't want her coming over her."

"It's a lil too late for that sweetheart." Kris says.

Mrs. Betty was heading in my direction, and I was ready for whatever energy she wanted to throw my way, but I was going to keep it cute. I was sizing her up as well. Noel was a good man, too good to be true even. Afterall he was a product of Mrs. Betty.

"Miss Amora, may I have a word with you honey?" she asked in her soft-spoken voice.

"Absolutely." I say as I stand up. I'll be back in a minute." I tell my girls before going off with Mrs. Betty.

She takes me to a high bar table. "You may not know this but it's not every day that my Noel introduces a woman to us. You must be some kind of special for my baby to bring you to a family event." She says with a smile. "I'm just amazed every time I look at you. You are such a gorgeous young woman."

"Thank you." I blush.

"I love your accent. Where are you from?"

"New Orleans."

"So where did the two of you meet."

"Noel and I met at Perry's Steakhouse & Grille in the Park District. He literally ran into me, busy looking in his phone." I say with a chuckle thinking back on the moment.

"I see. I see. What kind of work do you do? You dress well so you have to be making a pretty penny. Do you have any kids?"

"I'm a project manager at Sawyer Engineering Inc. No, I don't have any kids."

"A project manager?!" She asked with both shock and excitement in her tone. "You seem like such a girly girl. What made you choose construction as a career?"

"My dad was a carpenter before he died so I just kinda gravitated to construction to feel closer to him."

"Oh sweetie, I'm so sorry to hear that. Forgive me for asking."

"Thank you. It's not as hard on me as it used to be."

"Baby all we can do is pray and ask God for the strength we need to keep going. What about your mom? Does she live out here as well?"

"No mam. She didn't want to leave the city and I needed to get away."

"I understand. When Noel told me that he was moving to Dallas, I was heartbroken, but I knew he needed a change as well. Well sugar, I don't want to keep you away from your sister and friend for too long, but I enjoyed talking with you baby. I'm sure Noel told you that I didn't have any daughters. I would love for you to be the woman that changes that." she says with a smile and wink as she heads back to her seat, next to Mr. Nathan.

I'm still standing at the table when Noel sneaks up behind me and kisses my neck. I giggle. "Don't do that here." I say playfully turning around to face him.

"Why not?"

"Your parents are here."

"And?"

Noel wraps his arms around me and interlocks his fingers behind my back. "Would it be foolish of me to tell you that I'm falling in love with you?"

"Not at all. I literally fell for you the day we met." I laugh.

I caught you though. He says with a chuckle.

"Isn't that what you're supposed to do." I say looking Noel directly in his eyes. He kisses me. He kisses me like we weren't in a yard full of people.

Nathan taps Noel on his back to get his attention and when he does, he asks Noel who the girls were sitting at the fire pit. He tells him that the girls were with me. Nathan shrugs as if to say he didn't care.

"It doesn't matter who they came with." He says looking at me. "When you said your girl was bringing her friends, you didn't say they were that fine."

"They're both single Nathan if that's what you want to know." I tell him as I laugh. I look at Noel who's still holding me. "Your brother is a trip."

"Pack your bags baby."

We both watch as Nathan walks over to Kris. She looks over at me and I shrug. Angela sits there looking like a proud big sister, but I knew that she was waiting for her turn. It didn't take her long at all. Norman went to sit next to her soon after Kris was whisked away by Nathan. This was all in our plan. The fellas just didn't know it yet. I was going to put my sisters on. All three of these Brown men were handsome.

"Hey Mrs. Betty and Mr. Nathan. You look cute Mrs. Betty. Someone said very loudly as if they were on the other side of the yard.

"And there's Noble's girlfriend. You believe me now?" Noel says sarcastically.

Noble steps in the yard a few minutes later and head straight to Noel. I could tell that he was all the brothers' favorite brother. They all looked to him for advice. I knew this because of the many calls and texts he received from them the times we were together. After they give each other their brotherly handshake Noel introduces us.

"Nice to meet you, Amora."

"You too as well." I shake his hand.

"Why do I have to tell you to stop leaving me by myself?" The loud voice says as she walks over to the three of us.

"Amora, Tia. Tia, Amora." Noble introduces us.

"Hi Tia."

"What kind of name is Amora?"

"It's an elegant name. Something you have no clue about." Mrs. Betty says from behind me. "Noble get that girl away from my future daughter in law with this nonsense.

"I'm sorry Momma. She had a couple drinks before we came over. I'll talk to her."

"Teach her some class." Mrs. Betty says as she storms off.

Minutes later Mr. Nathan calls all his sons to the middle of the yard. They do as they're told.

"As some of you may know and to those that don't, I passed down the family business to my sons. My brothers and I started this company over 30 years ago with very little money in our pockets. I was the only one out of the three of us to be blessed with kids. I've always wanted boys so that I could pass the company down. As you all could see, I had four handsome boys. Now they're all men. Although, they may still act like boys from time to time." He says jokingly, binging on a few laughs. "But they've certainly grown into some fine men. I want you boys to know that your mom and I are truly proud of each of you, and we'd like to be the first to congratulate you. We love you boys and congratulations."

Everyone applauds Mr. Nathan for his beautiful speech. We watch as all the guys hug their parents and each other. The DJ plays "Celebration" by The Game featuring Chris Brown, Tyga, Wiz Khalifa, and Lil Wayne. The girls and I drank our wine that Noel poured for us just before the speech. I watched as all the guests surrounded the guys with excitement. Mrs. Betty made her way to me from the crowd. "It was so nice to meet you baby. We're about to head on back home before it gets too late." Mrs. Betty kisses my cheek then disappears.

We left the party a little while after sunset. The temperature had dropped, and I hated to be cold. Nathan had moved the party inside, but there were still too many people to fit them all in the house comfortably. He was disappointed to learn that Kris was leaving as well. She told him that she came with her sister, so she was leaving with her sister. That has been our pact since we were teenagers. Noel and I walked Kris and Angie to their cars then we headed out.

Since the ride to my house was a little over an hour, I told Noel that he could just grab some clothes and stay by me. I didn't want him to have to drive back home so late. I was considerate like that. Plus, I just wanted a little alone time with him since I didn't get much at the party. He happily accepted my offer and stopped home first to pack a bag. I loved to watch this man walk. Everything about him was sexy.

Chapter 9

Sunday morning when I woke up my body felt like lead. I was so stiff, and it hurt. Noel was still asleep, so I didn't bother him. I forced myself out of bed and into the bathroom to take a shower. Mid shower Noel walks into the bathroom.

"Morning beautiful." He says while urinating.

"Good morning."

"You mind if I join you?"

"Not at all." I say with a forced smile.

Noel gets in the shower, but my body is too exhausted to stand. Let alone have sex. He wraps his arms around me from behind and kisses my neck.

"Babe, my body hurts." He turns me around.

"What? Why?" He asks so innocently.

I shrug. "I don't know. That's why I'm taking this hot shower. Hopefully it'll loosen up."

"How about you soak instead of a shower. Soaking always helps relax your muscles."

I turn the shower off and wrap my towel around myself. I stop the tub up to run a bath. Noel finds my bubble bath and eucalyptus bath beads. He adds a little of each to my bath water. He even checks the temperature of the water. *"Could he be any more perfect?"* I thought to myself. "You soak and I'll get breakfast started." He kisses my forehand and heads for the kitchen.

I climbed into the tub and sat down to soak. The aroma itself was relaxing and the temperature of the water was perfect. I immediately felt a change in my body. As the bubbles grew higher and leveled with the rim of the tub, I turned the water off. I grabbed my eye mask from my basket and slid it on my face. I told Alexa to play my praise and worship playlist. The first song to play was *Stand Still by* The Walls Group. I got lost in the words and zoned out.

"Amora. Amora." Noel yelled and broke my trance. "Babe, you didn't hear me talking to you?"

"No, I'm sorry. What did you say."

"I was asking how long you were going to be because your breakfast was ready."

"Yea, no I didn't hear that at all." I say as I sit up in the tub. I unstop the tub and stand to take a shower. "Give me five minutes. I'll be out. Promise."

Satisfied that his question was answered, Noel left me alone in the bathroom. I took a quick shower and went to eat the breakfast that my man had cooked for me.

"What you have planned for today?" Noel asked me.

"Nothing really. Probably read a few notes to catch up for work tomorrow. Why? What have you planned?"

"I'm going watch football with the bros. I was just asking because I didn't want to leave if you wanted to do something."

"Aww that's sweet but I'm fine. I've been busy all week. I'll use this day to relax."

"How your body feeling now?"

"Refreshed. That soak was just what I needed. I didn't even realize my body was exhausted."

"You never do when you're busy. Welp, football starts at twelve so I'm about to take a shower and head out."

"Okay." I finish my omelet and put my dishes in the dishwasher. I grab my briefcase, take a seat on the sofa, and pull out some progress notes to look over. Chuck's project just so happened to be the first on the stack. Although I had already read it, I read over it again to make sure I didn't miss anything. The extension he'd asked for was coming to an end soon. "I only demanded him to get rid of one person, not the entire crew. This slick bastard." I say out loud not realizing Noel had come into the living room.

"I'll call you later." Noel says then kisses me. I laid the papers down and grabbed the back of Noel's head. I stand up and wrap my arms around and kiss him some more. His kisses always made me wet and weak. He was definitely the one. I walked him to the door when we've had enough. He kisses my forehead and leaves.

Kris called me later in the evening to talk to me about Nathan. She said that he was an intelligent and handsome man, but he was a whore. I laughed because I had already gotten that vibe from him. She said that she wasn't going to be the fool that sits around to find out if she can change him. I didn't blame her. My girl was educated and beautiful. She said that Nathan tensed up when she told him what her profession was. I fell out laughing. He must've thought she was going to try and evaluate him.

Not long after I hung up with Kris, Angie called me. She told me that Norman had invited her out for dinner, and she didn't know what to wear. I told her to just put on a simple black dress and heels. She told me how nervous she was and how she didn't want him to know that she was a klutz. I suggested that she just be honest with Norman if the subject came up. She went on to get ready for her date and I continued with my reports.

Chapter 10

I walked into my office the next day to a giant bouquet of light pink and white roses. It was beautiful and they smelled fresh as if they had just been picked. I looked for a card but there wasn't one. I assumed they were from Noel, so I texted him to thank him.

Me: GM Noel. I just wanted 2 ty 4 my beautiful bouquet. It's very beautiful.

Noel: GM. Uh, yw.

Me: Y the uh?

Noel: The courier was 2 deliver them @ 9am. He got there early. Guess I should give him a good tip.

Me: Sounds like it. Well, I'm about to get on these reports. TTYL

Erica came into my office. "Ms. Scott, is there anything you need me to bring to the mail room? Do you need coffee or tea?"

"No thank you to both questions. I grabbed a smoothie on my way in."

"Great. Your boyfriend has expensive taste by the way." She says pointing to the flowers.

"Thank you. He's trying to spoil me, and I like it." I say jokingly. Erica giggles then leave to continue her mission. I did the same. These reports weren't going to write themselves. The courier showed up at 9am just like Noel said he would. *"If these are the flowers that Noel sent, then who sent these?"* I thought to myself. Thinking nothing of it I continued with my work. I spent half my day typing up reports and proofreading them. By lunch I was ready to head home until I got a surprise visit.

"Miss Amora? How are you today my baby?" I look up to see Mrs. Betty walking into my office.

"I'm doing well. What a wonderful surprise." I say as I get up from my seat. I give her a kiss on the cheek. "Would you like to sit down?" I asked while pulling out a chair for her. She sits.

"I'm sorry for popping up at your place of work but I insisted that I personally apologize to you for the way Tia acted on Saturday. You are a classy young woman, and she has no business acting the way that she does. We all tolerate her because Noble says he loves her. I don't know what he sees in that gold-digger." I sit in silence while she vents. "If I had my way, she would've been gone a long time ago. Nathan told me to stop trying to interfere with my boys' lives but they're my babies. My boys deserve good respectful women. That girl is loud and ignorant."

To change the direction of the conversation I ask, "I was about to grab lunch, would you care to join me?"

"Oh, I'd love to honey but Nathan is downstairs waiting for me. We're heading back to Houston.

"Rain check then?" I ask.

"Absolutely. I'd love a mother daughter day out with you." I helped her out of her seat.

"I'll ride the elevator with you and walk you to the car on my way out."

"You don't have to do that baby. You're so well mannered. I'm going to have to tell Noel to take you off the market immediately. You don't find any young ones like you these days."

Mrs. Betty made me think. Noel and I hadn't made anything official just yet. People say all kinds of stuff during sex, but I needed to know. I made a mental note to speak with Noel once I got off from work. While on the elevator Mrs. Betty was still going on about Noble's girlfriend Tia. When we made it downstairs, Mr. Nathan was standing in front of the building.

"How you doing, Mr. Nathan?"

"I can't complain, sweetheart. How are you?"

"I'm doing well. Thanks for asking. Ya'll travel safely. I'll have Noel check on you all later."

We parted ways and I headed home. I told Erica that I'd work the rest of the day from home on my way out. Just as I made it inside my condo my cell phone rang. My hands were full, I couldn't answer. It rang again. Once in my condo I tossed everything on the sofa and checked my phone. Three missed calls from Noel. I called him back.

"Is everything okay?" I ask when he answers.

"I was wondering the same thing. My mom called me demanding that I call you. I thought something was wrong."

I laugh. "Yea, she's trying to get you to take me off of the market."

"I thought I already established that."

"Yea, about that. We should talk."

"What are you doing right now?"

"I'm home. I'm completing the rest of my day here at home."

"I'm on my way."

"I'll be here." We hang up. I went into my fridge to see what I had to eat. Nothing. I didn't feel like cooking anything. I decided to take a nap instead. My mind was overworked and needed a little time off.

Noel rang my bell close to 2pm causing me to jump out of my sleep. I had fallen asleep on the sofa. Something that I rarely did. I must've been really tired. I opened the door and put on a big smile.

"Hey you." Noel says as he picks me up as he walks in. He closes the door with his foot, and I lock it while he kisses me like he missed me. "Let's talk." He says as he puts me back on my feet.

"Oh, you want to get straight to the point. I like it."

"The best way to do business."

I blush. "You told me that you wanted me to be yours, but you have not officially made me your girlfriend. Your woman. Sex does not make you entitled to me in any way, shape or form."

He nods. "Amora, would you do me the honor of being my woman?"

"I'd have to think about it." I say with a smile. Noel picks me up off my feet and starts to kiss me. He carries me to my bedroom and lays me onto the bed. "Babe, I'm starving."

"You haven't had lunch?"

"No.

"Want to go to Open Palette?"

"Sure."

Noel drove us to the restaurant while I completed a zoom meeting that I had forgotten about. It was one of those meetings that Stephanie scheduled at the last minute. She was good for doing that. She had access to all of our calendars but never seemed to look at them when scheduling meetings. As Noel pulled into the garage, the valet opened my door to help me out of the car. Once we met up, Noel and I walked into the restaurant hand in hand.

"Welcome to Open Palette. How many?" The hostess asks as we walk up to the counter.

"Just the two of us." Noel responds.

"Would you like a booth or bar seat?

"We'd like a booth if it's not too much to ask.

"Right this way." She says as she leads us to an available booth. "Your waitress will be right with you."

"Thanks." I say before she walks away. "It's nice in here. Where do you find all these places?"

"We get invited to all sorts of places for business meetings. Restaurants, clubs, strip clubs, etc. I just take note of the places I want to revisit."

"When's your birthday?" I ask.

"December 14th."

"When's yours?"

"September 5th."

"Oh, you just had a birthday then. I understand you a little better now. We don't even know the simple things about each other." I nod. "I didn't need to. The chemistry was enough for me." Noel says.

"I turned thirty-two last month. My favorite color is blue. I love looking at the sky, mostly at night and I like to count the stars."

"I'll be thirty-four this December. My favorite color is blue as well —"

"My name is Rebecca. I'll be your server. Are there any drinks that I can get you?" The waitress says extra jolly as she approaches the table.

"I'll have a sprite and a glass of water."

"I'll have the same." Says Noel. Rebecca walks away. "Like I was saying, my favorite color is blue as well. I like making money. For fun I enjoy getting in a little COD every now and then."

"Do you have plans for your birthday?"

"Not at the moment. Will you be free?"

"I don't know. I just started my job so," I shrug. I'll figure something out though."

The waitress comes back with our drinks and take our meal orders. We both ordered a twelve-piece lemon pepper wings sharable with ranch dip. Another something that we had in common.

"I'm happy we talked. You can talk to me about whatever, whenever."

"I thought about it yesterday. The attraction is there but we didn't take the time to get to know each other before sex. Sex tends to complicate things."

"I agree but when I told you, you were mine I meant it. I wanted you from the moment I knocked you off your feet." We both laugh.

"I got your flowers this morning."

"I know, you told me that."

"No, after we got off the phone, the courier brought them at 9 like you said he would." He looks at me confused. "There wasn't a card with the other bouquet. I assumed you sent those also."

He shakes his head. "No babe, it wasn't me.

The food came and we ate in peace. Who could've sent those roses? I wondered.

Chapter 11

It was Thanksgiving Day, and I was spending it with Noel and his family. I asked my mom to fly to Dallas, but she declined my offer. Mrs. Betty was more than excited to have me over. Noel and I had ridden out the day before so that I could help Mrs. Betty cook. She loved my cooking. I made a pot of gumbo, a pan of cornbread dressing, and stuffed bell peppers. Mrs. Betty did all the baking.

For breakfast Mr. Nathan and Noel made a ton of food. They set up the dining room for a buffet style brunch. Pancakes, waffles, fried chicken, bacon, sausage, shrimp and grits, and mimosas. You name it. This was definitely the kind of tradition I wanted to pass down to my kids whenever I had some.

Dinner was scheduled for five in the evening, but people started coming at 3 and 4pm. To my surprise Kris came strolling in hanging on Nathan's arm.

"Well, well, well, what do we have here." I say as I chuckle. "I had no clue that this would be a family reunion."

"Girl shut up." Kris says jokingly as she hugs me and kisses my cheek.

"Nathan said that we should surprise you." Noel walks up behind me. "Hey Noel."

"What's up Kris?" He says as if they were buddy buddy.

"So, you knew about this?" I asked him.

"Of course, I did." Noel says with a chuckle. "Nathan is my brother."

"Let me guess. Angie's going to pop up here with Norman?"

"Hey, it wasn't my business to tell."

I follow Noel through the foyer and whisper, "And my body's not your business to touch." I playfully stick my tongue out at him before I join everyone else in the living room. Noble and Tia hadn't made it to the house yet. Noel told me earlier in the day that they were going to visit Tia's parents first. It was my plan to eat dinner and head back to the hotel.

As it got closer to five, I started getting the guest to move to the dining room. Mrs. Betty and I had already set the table beforehand. The food was all there waiting to be plated.

Mr. Nathan said a short prayer to bless the meal we were about to receive. Then we all ate.

"Excuse me for a minute if you may." Said Mrs. Betty. "I know I've probably introduced her to you all already, but I want you all to meet my sweet Amora. She's Noel's future wife. They aren't engaged yet, but I can feel it in my soul. Many years ago, we used to stand and tell the table what we were thankful for." She chuckles. "I won't force you all to do that today." Everyone let out a sigh of relief. "But I do want to tell you all that I am thankful for each and every one of you. Amora baby I am especially thankful for you on this day. Although your mom couldn't come to visit, you still catered to me and made sure I had everything that I needed. You took the strain off of me this year and I thank you."

"It was my pleasure Mrs. Betty. I'd do it all again if I had to." I said shyly. I was put on the spot and all eyes were on me. I needed someone to take the spotlight off me. No one did. Instead, I asked, "If you're done you can just leave your plates where they are. I'll get them." The men crowd back in front of the television to watch whatever game was on.

As I was removing the dishes and food from the table Kris came in to help me. "I can't believe your ass didn't tell me you were coming."

"I didn't really decide until Tuesday night."

"Aww, Nathan must've dicked you down some good to get you to come out here. I said laughing.

"Oh baby, Noel must've done the same to you cause yet here you are." She says as she playfully pushes me.

"Shhh girl. Mrs. Betty might hear you." We both look around then back at each other and laugh. "You know she thinks I'm innocent.

"She's such a sweetheart."

"She is."

"See Noble, I told you that they were going to eat without us. You were acting like you was too good to eat by my momma." Tia walks into the kitchen yelling. She wasn't actually yelling but I don't think anybody ever taught her how to use her inside voice.

"It's time to go. I told Noel I wasn't dealing with her voice all night." I say to Kris.

"I got a headache soon as I heard 'see Noble.' We both laugh. I walked into the kitchen to start the dish washer but instead I overheard Tia flirting with Noel.

"I bet she can't ride that big dick like I can. You better ask about me. I give the best head, ask your brother." She says just above a whisper.

I signaled for Kris to go around to the other entrance of the kitchen. I wanted to box Tia's ass in the kitchen. I stood in the doorway and waited until Kris walked around to where Noel was before saying something. To Kris I said, "So the hoe does know how to use her inside voice."

"I see." Said Kris.

I walked towards Tia. "And where the fuck do you think I'll be while you're riding his big dick and how do you know how big his dick is?" I ask her as I begin to take my hoop earrings out of my ears.

"Babe." Noel says to get my attention.

Still walking towards Tia, Noel gets in between us, I say, "Don't babe me. Answer my question hoe."

Noel called Noble to the kitchen in his big brother voice. Mr. Nathan and Mrs. Betty must've caught the urgency in his voice because they came also.

"Sister-in-law I was just playing with him. I don't want your man. I have my own man." She says looking around.

"What's going on Noel?" Noble asked.

"Your hoe of a girlfriend just told Noel that she can, excuse my language Mrs. Betty and Mr. Nathan, ride his big dick better than Amora can." Said Kris.

"She said what?!" Noble yells. "Oh, baby girl it's time for you to go.

"Noble, they're lying on me, baby. She's lying."

"Tia, I knew you were trouble the day my son brought you home." Mrs. Betty said in her soft-spoken voice. She couldn't raise her voice if she wanted to.

"Mrs. Betty, you ain't never liked me but soon as Noel brought her snotty ass around your nose has been up her ass. I was here first." She said as she started crying.

"Get the fuck out of my parents' house Tia!" Noble said as he slammed his fist on the countertop.

I moved away from Noel and went to the guestroom where all of our things were. Kris followed me. "You can just leave with me and Nathan."

"I'm about to get a Lyft to my hotel. I'll just rent a car to get back home."

"Amora, I'll have Nathan bring you to the hotel. Don't start tripping now Mo."

I started to cry. "Kris, I asked her the question, but he didn't answer me either did he?"

"I know." She says as she hangs her head.

"I'm leaving."

I took my phone out of my pocket to reserve a Lyft. There was a driver seven minutes away, so I hurried to grab all of my bags and walked outside. Kris was on my heels, but she knew that she couldn't stop me. I needed to get away from this house. Noel's family. I needed to get back to Dallas. Noel came outside soon as the Lyft driver pulled up. I had no words for him. I got in the car and waited while the driver put my bags in the trunk.

Chapter 12

I sat on the porch with my head in my hands for hours after Amora left me. It wasn't anything anybody could've said or done to make me feel better. Tia was dead ass wrong. She let her ignorance get the best of her and sadly Amora was the price I had to pay. She not only disrespected me but also Amora. As well as herself and my mom. Neither of them deserved that. Amora told me on the way to Houston that she wanted to leave my parent's house once Tia got there. I should've listened.

My ride back to Dallas was a long quiet one. I spent the whole weekend trying to get ahold of Amora. She wouldn't answer my calls. She wasn't responding to messages. I didn't even know if she had made it back to Dallas. I went to her condo. Nothing. She was done with me, and I couldn't blame her. Kris told me after Amora left that she wanted an answer. I was too surprised myself to give her one. Tia had never come at me like that before. What she did was blatantly inappropriate. I hated her for it.

Noble must've apologized to our mom and I over a million times. It wasn't his fault. Tia had no sense of decorum. The girl was ignorant, and it was her choice to remain that way. No amount of money would've changed that. She had the resources that she needed to get help at her fingertips. Noble saw potential in her but not even that could save her after what she told our mom.

Every bouquet that I sent to Amora's office was rejected and sent back to me. I tried to go to her office, but security stopped me. She said that Amora asked that I never come or send anything to her office again. Still no calls nor texts. She was hitting the red button on me. All of my text said "Delivered." She wasn't reading them.

On Thursday, I received a call from a number that I didn't know. It was Tia asking if she could meet me for lunch. She said that she wanted to apologize to me in person for the trouble that she had caused. I hung up on her without agreeing. I called Noble and asked if he knew anything about her trying to meet with me. He told me that it was to my discretion. I slept on it. The next day I called her and told her that we could do lunch. I needed to be somewhere fully populated in case she tried to do something inappropriate.

We met at the Grill & Vine Restaurant in Downtown Dallas. I wondered what made her choose this particular spot because she lived more than an hour away. I walked into the restaurant and told the hostess that I was waiting for a common woman. She nodded as if she understood what I meant and led me to my table. Tia showed up more than ten minutes late. Loud as usual.

"Hey Noel. Oh, I'm so glad you could meet me today." She says as she takes a seat. "I was so devastated when Noble had put me out. I never meant no harm."

"What did you expect to happen? What made you make those comments that you made?"

"Well damn brother-in-law can't we at least order our food first? I'm starving. I've waited all morning for this."

We sit in silence until the waitress comes to get our orders. I order my drink and entrée at the same time. I was ready to get this apology meeting over with. I noticed that something was a little off with Tia, but I couldn't put my finger on it. Every few minutes she looked over her shoulder as if she was being followed. I didn't see anyone out of the ordinary.

"Damn brother-in-law that looks good." She says as the waitress places my fish tacos of front on me. She even had the audacity to stick her fork in my plate.

"Tia don't stick your fork in my food. Next time I won't be so nice."

"Damn, I just wanted to taste it."

"Then you should've ordered yourself some." I say with all of the sarcasm I could muster. "You said that you wanted to apologize. I'm listening." I was down to my last taco and Tia was on her second glass of wine.

"I do want to apologize to you." She says flirtatiously as she rubs my hand. I move my hand away from her. "Don't be like that Noel. I apologize for Amora hearing what I said but I don't apologize for saying it. You are a better man than Noble; you and I both know it. I deserve a man like you."

"You've got to be fucking kidding me." I rub my temple. "Tia there is nothing about you that attacks me to you." I say while getting up from my chair. Tia tries to get up as well but stumbles and falls back in her chair. "How much have you had to drink Tia?"

"Why you acting like you're worried now?"

"I'll go get you a room so you can sober up." I walked over to the receptionist desk at the hotel and reserved Tia a room for the rest of the day. I explained to the receptionist what was going on and told her to call Noble if she tried to leave before sobering up. She agreed and I tipped her $50. I walked back into the restaurant to get Tia who's now resting her head on the table. My blood started to boil. I was embarrassed. Not just for me but for Tia as well.

I picked Tia up from the chair and wrapped my arm around her waist. She could barely walk in the stiletto heels that she had on. Now that I was closer to her, I could smell more than just wine on her breath. She must've been drinking before meeting me. While we waited for the elevator, Tia wrapped her arms around me as if trying to keep herself balanced. As uncomfortable as I felt I didn't move her arms because it would've looked bad had I let her fall on the floor. To the public's eye, I looked like a black man trying to take advantage of an intoxicated woman.

We rode the elevator up to the room I got for Tia. I walked her to the door and opened it for her to walk in. She stumbled forward taking me with her. I ended up falling on top of her. To my surprise she grabbed my face and tried to kiss me. I smacked her hand away from my face. She smiled. I used the floor to push myself up and stood up. I grabbed Tia under her arms and dragged her to the bed. I left her intoxicated body stretched out across the bed. As I headed out, I reminded the receptionist of our deal. I called Noble on my way out to let him know where Tia was.

Since I was in the area I decided to go to Amora's condo and wait. I needed to see her. It had been over a week. I couldn't go empty handed, so I stopped at a floral shop on the way to get her some flowers. To my surprise her car was parked outside of the garage when I arrived there. I parked behind her to make sure she couldn't leave. I knocked on the door. There wasn't an answer. I went to her garage door and knocked.

After twenty minutes of knocking, ringing the bell and calling her phone, Amora finally opened the door. I walked in to see that she had been living in her living room. There were takeout containers all over the island and dining table. There were empty wine bottles and glasses everywhere. My love was hurt, and I saw it with my own eyes. "What do you want Noel?"

"We need to talk."

"Talk about what? HUH?!" She yells.

I closed and locked the door. "What's bothering you babe?"

"Right now, you. You're fucking bothering me. Didn't I leave your ass in Houston?" She sits on the sofa and pulls a pillow in her lap.

"You did but I want to know why? Tell me why you left."

"I left because had I stayed, I would've killed that bitch in your mom's house, and I didn't want to take it there. And tell me how the fuck the hoe knows how big your dick is?"

"Amora listen to yourself. You think I'd fuck my brother's girlfriend? What kind of nigga do you think I am? I'm a man babe. Give me my fucking credit please. Tia is a hoe. I'd never be desperate enough to fuck somebody like her or anyone else for that matter. I'm with you."

"You were with me that night too. You didn't even answer my question when I asked. You still haven't answered it. HOW THE FUCK DOES SHE KNOW HOW BIG YOUR DICK IS NOEL?"

"She doesn't babe." I say with a little anger in my tone. "How the fuck can you let this dumb ass hoe change what we have based off of some dumb shit she said? I'm with you, Amora. I always am. I go to work and I come back to you. You know this shit. I've never given you a reason to think or believe otherwise."

"Oh, so now you're upset. YOU?!" You didn't even follow me when I left the kitchen. You just stood your stupid ass there with the dumb hoe. You let me pack." She says as she begins to sob. I wrap my arm around her and pull her closer to me.

"Babe, I stayed to make sure that my mom was okay. She did disrespect my mom too, not just you."

"I know."

"Look at me." I say but she looks elsewhere. I gently turn her face towards me by her chin. "I love you. I'm not going anywhere, I told you that. And I don't want another woman. You're enough for me."

"I love you too."

And just like that we told each other those three words. I meant them. I meant everything that I'd ever told Amina. I was going to make her my wife. There was nothing another woman could do for me that she couldn't. She was my light at the end of a tunnel. She was my rainbow after a storm. I was madly in love with this woman.

Chapter 13

Thanksgiving night I had my Lyft driver take me to the nearest car rental place. I was able to reserve an economy car. From there I booked a hotel room at the Hilton for the night. I stayed there all-night crying and trying to figure out why I needed my question answered so badly. I knew that Tia was classless, and that Noel didn't find her attractive. Then it hit me, I was in love with Noel. I loved Noel.

Once I made it back to Dallas, I ordered a few bottles of wine through Doordash. I was in no shape to return to work just yet. I ordered in for a few days before finally deciding to go to the grocery store. Just as I was backing out of the garage Noel's location pinged to my phone. He was coming to my house. I put my car in park and ran back inside. He was the last person I wanted to see but he was also the only person I wanted to be around.

****

"I just told this man I loved him. What's wrong with me?" I thought to myself. He told me that I was enough for him, and I was hoping that he was right.

"Babe, you think you made enough of a mess?

I sighed. "Too soon Noel. Too soon."

"I'm just saying. It's looking like a wino lives here."

I get off of the sofa and go to my pantry for a trash bag to clean up my mess. Noel helped with the living room while I took on the dining and kitchen areas. I loaded the dishes into the dishwasher and mopped the floors. By the time we were done my condo smelled lemony fresh.

"I'm going to take a shower."

"I'll be here when you're done." Noel says.

Since he wanted to wait, I made him wait. I ran a bath to soak instead of just taking a shower. I poured in a little rose scented oil and a little bubble bath. "Alexa, play some 90's R&B." Soon as I put one foot in the tub Noel came walking into the bathroom.

"You said you were taking a shower not a bath."

"And you said that you'd wait. What happened to you waiting?" I ask, with my eyebrow raised.

"It's been over a week Amora."

"I know this."

Noel takes his clothes off and joins me in my bubble bath. "Why is this water so hot?"

"Don't get in here judging my water, you could've stayed on the sofa."

Noel eases down behind me as I turn the cold water on to please the crybaby. I wave the water around a little to help blend it. "You happy now crybaby?" I turned the water off.

"Yes I am." He says as he pulls me back against him. I laid the back of my head on his chest and mellowed out for a bit. Just to think I was going to let Tia make me lose out on a good man. I still wanted to fuck her up, but she wasn't worth it. My man was right here with me.

"I love you Noel." I say as I turn to become face to face with him. He then turns my body so that I'm straddling him.

105

"I love you too." Noel says then kisses me. He kisses me so hard I could've sworn I felt his tongue touch my tonsils. He squeezes my ass as he kisses my neck and breast. I moan in his ear as he nibbles on my breast, the left then the right. Noel gently slides his erection into my sweet spot. I let out a loud moan. "Ride this dick like you missed it." Noel says and I did just that. I wrapped my arms around his neck and bounced on his dick as hard and fast as I could. I missed him and he had me dickmetized.

"It feels so good." I whispered in Noel's ear.

"You riding this dick good too." Noel assured me that I was doing a good job but I was getting cramped in the small space. I stopped riding him and let the water out of the tub. I got out of the tub and led Noel to my bed. He laid me on my back and took me missionary style.

"That's my spot babe. That's my... Noel you're going to make me cum."

"That's the objective. Wet this dick up."

"Babe." I moan as I tighten my grip. "I'm cummin." I moan louder as my orgasm shoots from my body.

"Oh fuck." Noel says as he speeds up his rhythm and begins to grind harder with each plunge. "I know you got one more in you." He turns me on my belly. He spreads my ass cheeks as he slowly moves his dick in and out of my pussy.

"Please babe." I begged. "Don't stop."

"I'm not stopping until you cum for me again." Noel interlocks his hands with mine as he pushes deeper into me. I loved it. His dick was perfect. His dick was mine.

"That shit feels good babe." I moaned.

"You like that?"

"Yes."

"Tell me you like it."

"I like it babe. I like it." I started to flex my yoni muscles as Noel continued to move in and out.

"Oh fuck. I'm about to cum."

"Not yet." I say as I move for us to change positions. "I want to look at you when you cum."

Noel pushes my legs toward my head as he lays on top of me. He plunges into my pussy.

"Ohhh." I tightened my grip around his back. "I love you babe."

"I love you too." Noel slides his arms underneath my back and squeezes me tight. He grinds inside of me. I lose control. I was lost in his touch and kisses. I came so hard. Then Noel came. He collapsed next to me. "That's what happens when you make me wait a week."

"Now, I'm going to take a shower." I say with a chuckle.

Noel was still stretched out on the bed when someone rang the doorbell. "Babe, you expecting someone?" He yelled from the bed.

"No." I yelled back. I continued taking my shower. When I got out of the bathroom Noel wasn't in the bedroom anymore. I didn't see any of his clothes either. I grabbed my robe from behind my bedroom door and walked into the living room. Noel was standing at the island looking down at something. The closer I got to the island I noticed that it was a hotel room key.

"What's that?" I say as I get closer to Noel. Once I'd gotten closer, I noticed a piece of paper next to it that read:

I'M WATCHING YOU...

"What's this?" I say picking up the hotel room key. "I've never stayed at The Westin." I look at Noel for answers.

"Somebody must've been following me."

"What do you mean?"

"I was there earlier today. Before I came over here." He tells me. Feeling confused I could feel my facial expression change.

"What were you doing at the hotel?"

"Let me make a call first then I'll explain."

"NO! Explain this shit right now."

"Amora give me a minute." Noel pulls out his phone and makes a call. "Have you spoke with Tia since earlier?"

What the fuck does Tia have to do with the hotel key? I wondered. I needed answers and I needed them now.

"I'm over here with Amora and someone rang the bell but when I got to the door no one was there. They left the damn room key and a note taped to the door. I'll ask her but I never paid attention to be honest."

"Ask me what?" I said as I was getting more impatient by the second.

Noel put up a finger at me and I wanted to break that muthafucker off. I wanted to know what was going on and who the hell was watching me or him.

"So, she's still there? Can you call her to be sure? Call me back." He hangs up.

Chapter 14

After I had gotten off my call with Noble, I tried talking to Amora. She was angry as hell, and I couldn't be upset with her. Someone had followed me to her house, and I had no clue as to who it could've been. My mind was going a thousand miles a minute. I wanted to know who was following me but even more, so I needed to protect Amora.

"Tell me what the fuck is going on Noel."

"Tia called and asked me to meet her at Grill & Vine for lunch. She claimed she wanted to apologize to me in person for all of the trouble she caused me. I knew it sounded fishy but Noble said meeting her couldn't hurt so I did. Anyway, we ate but then she seemed really drunk so I booked her a room. To sober up"

"I'm assuming at The Westin?"

"Yea, we were already there. The restaurant is located inside of the hotel."

"I don't get it though. You booked her a room and what else?"

"I called Noble, told him that I'd put her up in a room and then I came here."

"That's it!"

"Babe that's it. Nothing happened."

"Did that bitch follow you to my house Noel because I will kill her?" Amora questions. Then my phone rings. It's Noble.

"Hold up. Yeah." I say as I answer the phone.

"I just spoke to her. She said she was literally about to call me. Something about she may have drunk too much before meeting with you. She said she's sorry for behaving that way by the way but she was nervous. Either way it couldn't have been her that brought the note. Her location is still at the hotel. No way she would've made it back that fast bro."

"That's true. I need to figure this shit out and fast."

"Well, you know where to find us if you need us." Noble says.

"Let me talk with Mo and I'll hit you up later."

"Cool." We hung up.

"So?" Amora asks soon as I look in her direction.

"It wasn't Tia."

"Who the hell was it then? They know where I live Noel." Amora says more panicked than before.

"Whoever it was had to follow me here. I've been here for hours though." I say as I scratch my head. "You have a security system, right?"

"Yea." She pulled up her cameras on her phone but the only thing that we could see was a person in dark clothes wearing a hoodie. The camera never caught their face. From the build I assumed it was a guy but why would a guy be following me to Amora's house. "That looks like a man Noel."

"I was thinking the same thing."

"This is insane. Why would a guy follow you to my house and what the hell does this note mean? I have so many questions." Amora starts to pace in the living room of her condo.

"Look, you can come stay by me for a few days, but it'll be a commute getting back and forth to work." I suggested.

"What if he knows where you live too?"

"There's only one way to find out." I speak. "Let's hope that whoever it is doesn't make the mistake of popping up at my house."

Within the next hour Amora was rolling her luggage into the living room. She had damn near the full set packed with God knows what. I was speechless.

"I'm ready." She said.

"Did you pack your whole closet?" I asked jokingly.

"No, I did not." She responded and rolled her eyes. "I packed enough for a week."

"Babe, you have four suitcases and a garment bag."

"Uhm yea, my work clothes and coats are in the garment bag." She says holding it out in front of me. "My shoes are in a suitcase. My regular clothes are in a suitcase. My accessories are in a suitcase. I don't know about you, but I take care of my valuables."

"Amora, you don't need any clothes, you're coming to stay with me. Just get your toothbrush." I say as I stand and wrap my arms around her waist. I kiss her on her forehead. "I'll start putting your things in the car."

"Yea you do that. I'll double check to make sure I'm not leaving anything."

Chapter 15

The day after the stalker fiasco I had a zoom meeting with my supervisor Jake. I wanted to give him an update on what was going on and why I had preferred to work from home the upcoming week. He told me that he would have lobby security check the visitation logs and send him copies. Jake was the best supervisor that I had ever had. He was genuinely concerned about all of his employees.

He told me that with the cold weather and icy roads most of the office staff were working from home anyway. We went over a few notes for a couple of projects we had in the works. I sent him the progress notes that had been emailed to me from one of the contractors. Their project had been delayed due to materials being on backorder. We made plans to take a trip out to our project sites on a warmer day.

After I got off of the zoom meeting with Jake, I ordered a few groceries online to be delivered. I hated being cold so the less trips outside I had to make the happier I was. I was going to make Noel and I some seafood stuffed chicken breast served with some creamy garlic pasta and a side garden salad. It was the least I could do since I was staying at his house for the whole week.

While I waited for the food to be delivered, I watched a couple of movies and did a little bit of exercising. I do mean a little bit. I'd planned on doing a hundred squats, but I couldn't take anymore after sixty-one. I drank a bottle of water and headed for the shower. The food still hadn't made it by the time I'd gotten out.

I decided to call Noel and see how his day at work was going. He acted like he just had to go to the office this morning for some reason. He answered on the first ring. "This is Noel."

"I know who you are."

"Hey you. You called my business phone."

I looked at the contact and realized he was right. "You want me to call your personal phone?"

"You're fine. What you up to?" He asks me as if he couldn't see me through the security system.

"I look at the camera and say, "You're asking as if you can't see me sitting here."

"I'm not spying on you. You must think I'm a creep." He says jokingly.

The bell rings. "Babe who's at the door?"

"It's a young lady holding grocery bags. She's in a lime green Kia Soul."

"But you're not spying on me. I say as I roll my eyes. I'll wait till she leaves." I tell Noel.

"You being anti-social today?"

"No, I just don't want to talk to anybody." I say sarcastically. The bell rings again.

"Just go answer the door, she's not leaving."

I grabbed my coat from the coat rack on my way to the door. The lady rings the bell again. "Just a minute." I yelled out. I unlocked the door to find her standing there holding the bags. I'm sorry. I thought you'd just leave them."

"I was going to but then your neighbor gave me this to give to you." The young lady says pointing in the direction of the corner.

She hands me an envelope with my name on it. I look around to see if someone else sees us. I hurried to take the bags and put them inside. I then closed the door and walked to the sidewalk to see if I'd see anything unusual. I didn't. In a state of panic, I had forgotten that Noel was on the phone and watching me the whole time. I speed walk back inside and lock the door.

"Amora!" I heard Noel yell into my ear.

"Yeah, I'm here. I'm here."

"I'm on my way."

"Ok." We ended the call. I went back to make sure that I had locked the door. I did. I knew Noel had cameras surrounding his house, but I was still uneasy. None of his neighbors knew my full name, if they knew me at all. The envelope said "*Ms. Scott.*"

I took the bags to the kitchen and with my back to the camera I opened the envelope. It was a picture of Noel on top of a woman with her legs wrapped around his legs. I could see that he was dressed but from the picture the female's dress was raised above her panties. I only knew it was Noel because I knew him from behind, from the build of his body to the back of his head. I couldn't make out where the picture could've been taken or who the female was.

All I knew was my man was laying on top of a woman with her dress up in this picture I held in my hand. I couldn't tell if he was kissing her or anything. It didn't even matter. I wanted to know how whoever gave her the envelope knew to find me here. I was being followed but by who. I was still fairly new to Dallas. I didn't hang out alone. I didn't have any enemies in Dallas. None that I knew of anyway.

Noel said he was on his way, but I didn't care. I wanted to be by myself. I called Kris to tell her about all of the creepy shit that had be transpiring. She asked if I had spoken to Mel and to be honest the thought never crossed my mind. I told her that I'd call her back later and called Mel.

She answered. "What's up Mo?"

"Someone's stalking me, +and I have no idea who it can be. They left a hotel room key taped to my door —"

"Slow down Amora. Somebody's stalking you?"

"Yes! Yesterday some guy taped a hotel room key to my door with a note saying, 'I'm watching you.' Turned out

Noel had been at the hotel. A story for another day. Anyway, so Noel thought it'll be best if I stayed with him for a few days. Now I'm here. I had groceries delivered today and the lady told me that a neighbor gave her an envelope for me. It had my name on it. Ms. Scott. Why would Noel's neighbors know my last name? That's absurd."

"So, this happened twice, as in two days in a row?"

"Yes. Somebody's been watching the both of us Mel and I don't know who it could be."

"What was in the envelope?"

"A picture of Noel lying on top of some woman."

"WHAT?!" Mel says as she chuckles. "I'm not laughing because it's funny. I'm laughing because that had to mean that someone was there with him and the woman. How would he not know who took the picture?"

"He hasn't seen the picture yet. He was at work when I got it."

"Shoot me yours and Noel's addresses, I'll have a couple of my guys to check some things for me. We'll definitely get to the bottom of this. Meanwhile, go get you some target practice. I know you don't like guns but now it's time to let that go." Mel says with seriousness in her tone.

I groan. "I have no choice at this point. It doesn't seem like I'm safe here or at home for that matter."

"You think he's cheating?" Mel quietly asks me. "I hope he's not but you never know."

"To be honest Mel, I don't believe he is but I'm not stupid either." We disconnect the call.

Chapter 16

Noel made it home not long after I finished my call with Mel. He came in frantic looking me over and asking if I was ok. I told him that I was fine and that I had everything handled. I explained to him that I had spoken to Mel and that she said she would have some guys pounding the pavement for me. Then I had to check him. "Explain to me what happened at the hotel."

"Huh? Noel asked surprised. What you mean? I told you everything."

"Did you go to the room with Tia or did you happen to meet someone else there?"

"Meet somebo —. No, I didn't meet anybody. Yes, I took Tia's drunk ass to the room."

"You conveniently left that part out the first time you told me the story. Why?"

"I told you I told Noble I was putting her up in a room to sober up."

"Yes, that's what you said. You didn't say that you went to the room with her." I folded my arms and frowned. "What else did you conveniently leave out? That you slept with her?"

Noel frowns and throws his hands up in frustration. "I did not have sex with Tia, Amora. I took her to the room, opened the door and she fell causing me to fall with her so basically, I fell on top of her. Then I got up picked her up and put her in the bed. I left right after that. Nothing else happened."

"I'm going back to my condo. I'd be safer there." I said as I walked towards the bedroom.

"Wait Amora. What are you talking about? You're going back to the condo because I cared about the safety of my lil brother's girlfriend?"

"NO, that's not why! You looked me square in my face and lied to me so effortlessly Friday. You told me nothing happened and I believed you Noel. You've literally added two incidents that you conveniently forget to mention. You must think I'm a damn fool. If you could omit "nothing," then how can you expect me to believe you're not hiding anything else?"

"Babe, I didn't do anything with that girl. Where is this coming from anyway?"

"There was a picture in the envelope. A picture of her dress above her waist and you on top of her." I looked towards the counter where I left it. Noel followed my eyes and walked to the counter. I went to the bedroom to get my things together.

"This is bullshit. You don't have to leave Amora."

"I need to. I think we need a break. Slow things down a little bit. At least until Melanie gets to the bottom of it because right now I'm feeling like you're the reason I'm being targeted."

"I'm going to get to the bottom of this Amora. I just need a little time. You know I wasn't with another woman."

"That could be true, you wasn't with another woman, you were with Tia. Your brother's girlfriend. I believe that we need a little space in between us to figure this out."

"What do you need from me Amora? Ask me anything. What is it that you need me to do?"

"I need you to help me put my things in my car." He did.

We hugged and kissed before I left. I watched him in the rearview until I could no longer see him. It took everything in me not to cry in front of him. I had no idea what I was going to do once I got home. What I did know was that I would've been a lot more comfortable in my own place. I needed to figure out if whoever this psycho was wanted to get back at Noel for something or if I was really the target.

The rest of the week was a blur for me. I went back to the office, but everything was kind of slow. Most of the time I sat at my desk browsing the web. Mel hadn't found out who the guy was yet. Noel and I barely spoke, and I wasn't really bothered by that. All I knew was that I needed some time alone to think. I needed to come up with a game plan. I needed a strategy to beat the stalker. I refused to walk around paranoid.

Monday following, I met a guy named Curtis at the coffee shop in the lobby. I'd just happened to run downstairs for a cup of hot chocolate. Curtis was well dressed and very polite. We talked a bit while we stood in line waiting for our orders. He told me that he had just started a job with a company on the third floor. I told him how lucky he was to be so close to the first floor. Having to take the stairs for fire drills was nothing nice. We laughed at the idea of all of the women having to take the stairs wearing high heels. After we got our orders, we parted ways.

"Ms. Scott?"

Erica buzzed me as soon as I made it back to my desk. "Yes, Erica?"

"There's a Mr. Curtis for you on line 1."

"You can transfer him."

"Great."

The call comes through. "Hello Mr. Curtis." I say as I answer the phone.

"It took me about three calls and a few transfers to finally get to you. No one knew who I was talking about when I asked for Amora."

"Most of the time I give my last name. I try not to get too personal with those I work with. I try to keep it as professional as possible. I've had a few bad experiences. You can't be nice to some people. Can't make friends at work."

"I can agree with that."

"It's not always bad but it's better to be safe than sorry." I said to sound less anti-social.

"True but also, some people just take their jobs to their heads. They like to go on a power trip when they have a position of authority."

Unsure of where that comment came from I just said, "Yea and that too."

"Well, I don't want to hold you up at work. I just wanted to hear your voice again before I left the office. It was really nice to meet you."

"Same here. Well now you know where to find me." I said even though I was a little repulsed he went through so much to call me. We disconnected the call.

The fact of Curtis going through all of the trouble of trying to find me was sweet, but it was also frightening. I knew that men appreciated the chase, but he was doing a little too much in my opinion. Maybe I just wasn't used to a guy going through all of the hassle. I needed a distraction and Curtis was going to be just that. Noel was on my mind heavy and his birthday being near didn't help not one bit.

I left the office around noon to work the rest of the day from home. It started snowing and I wanted to get home before it got too bad. I informed Erica to take a message if Curtis called and not to give him any of my contact information. She said, "I'm way ahead of you. Something about him seemed a little off to me if you know what I mean." Erica was an amazing assistant. She didn't get nearly as much credit from the rest of the office that she deserved. I smiled and went on with my day.

Chapter 17

Something felt a little off when I pulled into my driveway, so I decided to sit in the car for a few minutes. I texted Noel telling him I

missed him and thought that he should come over ASAP so we could talk in person. He responded and asked that I give him about twenty minutes, he was finishing up some paperwork. I responded that that was fine and proceeded to get out of my car.

The punch came out of nowhere, it landed right on my cheek bone. It was so powerful that I stumbled backwards onto my car. I felt a burning sensation in my jaw which caused me to cry out, but I couldn't open my mouth to scream. I was dazed and couldn't fight back. The guy grabbed me by my hair and slammed my head into my car. I cried. He kicked me more times than I could count. Blood started to pour from my mouth. I began to see stars just before my eyes became too heavy to keep open. I was losing consciousness.

When I woke up I saw bright lights and a bunch of people I didn't know. I couldn't make out who they were at first. I tried to move my arm, but it was too heavy. I tried to get someone's attention, but I couldn't speak. With my other hand I reached up to my mouth. My jaw felt tight, and I finally knew the reason. My jaw had been broken. My face was swollen. I turned my head as far as I could to see if there was someone close to me that I could tap.

As I reached, I could feel someone grab my hand. It was a young woman. Maybe a few years younger than I was. She asked if I needed something. All I could do was nod my head. I gestured with my left hand for a pen. She understood what I was trying to say and handed me a pen and notepad. I tried to write, "What happened?" but it came out too messy. She began guessing to figure out what I was trying to write.

Once I gave her a nod to let her know she'd guessed correctly, she moved close to my ear as if trying not to let the others hear and said, "some guy claiming to be your boyfriend brought you in here and stated that he found you lying outside of your home. He said someone must've tried to rob you. He's still here, he's in the waiting room. I can get him if you'd like." I

131

shake my head. "We've contacted the police, and they will be in shortly to speak with you. I nodded my approval. She apologized that someone was cruel enough to do what they did to me.

I heard, "I want to see her now! Where is she? What's taking them so long?" It was Noel's voice. The nurse looked back at me for confirmation. I nodded. I saw tears fall from Noel's eyes as he walked closer to me. I guess I looked as bad as I felt. It was bad enough that my jaw was broken but it was also hard for me to breathe. I began to cry too. Noel wiped the tears from my eyes as he assured me, he'd find who did this to me. He pulled a chair closer to my bed and sat down.

"I called everybody. Your sisters, my brothers, your mom, and my parents. I'm not risking you being left alone again. I will find who did this and make them regret it, you hear me?" I nodded, trying not to cry any harder because it hurt. "Your nurse told me that a guy claiming to be your boyfriend brought you in. The police would probably show you a line up. Would you be able to point him out? Do you remember anything?" I took my notepad and wrote that I only saw his eyes. "We'll find who did this to you, trust me."

Kris was the first one out of the girls to arrive. She was on the phone with Mel when she walked in. I knew this because I heard her ask Mel where her guys were when I was attacked. "I just walked into her room. I'll see you when you get here." She ended the call and dropped her phone into her purse. "Hi Noel." She said as gave him a one arm hug. "Any updates?"

"No updates since I last spoke with you." Noel stood up, giving Kris the seat. "They were taking her for imaging when I got here. They had me wait in the waiting room until she woke up. The doctor said, 'her jaw is broken and two of her left ribs are fractured along with a whole lot of bruising.' Whoever did this beat her badly. This was done out of pure hate."

"Where were you? How did you know she was here?"

"I was at the office when she texted me saying she wanted to talk. By the time I made it to there, it was too late. I found her phone and keys on the ground by her car. I knew then that something was off, that something had happened to Amora. I came to Parkland because it was the closest hospital. Kris, I'd never do anything to hurt her." Noel says.

Kris squeezes his hand. "No, no. I'm not insinuating anything, Noel. I would never accuse you of doing something

133

like this to her. I'm just trying to put the puzzle together. The timeline you know. That's my sister lying there. Erica said she had left work around noon. This had to have taken place soon after that." Kris looked at her watch. "It's 4:12pm now. Someone had to have followed her home. You guys have been being stalked for a few weeks now. Any idea of who it could possibly be?"

"No clue. I can't help but feel like this is my fault. I never should've let her go back to her condo. I should've fought harder to make her stay with me at my place." In unison they both say, "She's stubborn." Then they chuckled.

A detective is escorted into my room by the young nurse from earlier. The nurse says, "She can't talk at the moment, but I did give her a notepad to use. The doctor wants her to rest her jaw."

"Thank you. I won't hold her too long."

"Oh, it's okay. She's been a good patient. I just hope that you all find who did this to her."

"I pray that we can." The Detective said as he turned to Kris and Noel. He reached out his hand to shake their hands. "My name is Detective Lee. Can you tell me the dynamics of your relationship to our victim?"

"Hi, Kristine. I'm her sister and this is her fiancée, Noel."

"From what the nurse told me, she was brought in by her boyfriend."

"She's not seeing anyone else." Noel says. I can see his jaw clenching.

Sensing Noel's frustration Detective Lee said, "Okay, let me say this. I will say and ask a lot of uncomfortable things. It's all formality. It's all a part of doing my job. I need the both of you to help me help her. I'm here to help her in any way that I can. With that said, tell me everything you know."

Noel says, "She texted me at about 12:30pm. She said that she wanted to talk in person. I told her that I was finishing up paperwork and asked if she could give me twenty minutes. Once I made it to her condo, I found her belongings scattered on the ground but she was nowhere to be found. I saw blood next to her car. Her phone and keys were on the ground a few feet away from the car."

"Do you have those items with you now?" Detective Lee asks.

"Yes, I do." Noel reached in his suit pocket for the phone and keys. He reached both to the Detective. "I know the passcode if you need it."

"I'll get that from you a little later. I don't need the keys. It's standard procedure to go through calls and messages in hopes to find anything that stands out. Something that can help us with a lead. You can go on."

"Once I collected her items, I hurried to the closest hospital hoping that I'd find her. Here I am."

"Thank you for that. Ms. Kristine, when was the last time you'd heard from her?"

"Yesterday. We try to call or text each other every day. Our Mondays are always busy, so we usually talk after work. What I do know though, is that she left work at noon. I called her assistant right after Noel called telling me something happened to her."

"That was some detective work." Detective Lee said with a chuckle.

"Well, she's my sister. I had to put the timeline together. Also, someone had been stalking Amora and Noel for a few weeks now. Amora told us that she would handle it." She said then looked at me with a sarcastic expression on her face. "As we all could see, she didn't handle it. Being stubborn."

"Wait a minute. Wait a minute. You guys have been getting stalked?" He looked at Noel with a questioning expression.

"A week after Thanksgiving someone taped a keycard from a hotel onto the door of Amora's home." Detective Lee raises an eyebrow. "No, it wasn't anything like that. For Thanksgiving my former sister-in-law said some disrespectful things to my family and me. She asked that I meet her for lunch at The Westin to apologize in person. The sister-in-law. She had a few drinks and could barely walk straight. I booked her a room for her to sober up and escorted her to the room.

"I see."

"Afterwards I went to see Amora. Hours after I had been with her at her place someone rang the doorbell. That's when I found the keycard taped to the door. No one was outside. We watched the video footage. The person was masked and wearing all black."

"Was this the only incident?"

"No. I told her to pack her things so she could stay with me a few days. At least until we found out what was going on. The very next day she ordered groceries. I watched her through my Ring camera while the delivery woman was dropping off the groceries. We were on the phone as well. The delivery woman said that one of my neighbors had given her an envelope to give to Amora." Detective Lee nodded. "Only problem we had with that was, none of my neighbors knew Amora by her name. I watched as Amora walked to the curb in the direction the woman told her the neighbor went."

"Where do you live?" Detective Lee asks.

"I live in Little Elm."

"That's a little over an hour away, isn't it?

"Correct."

"What was in the envelope?" Detective Lee asks.

"It was a picture from the same event I mentioned. That's how Amora ended up back at home. She wanted to put some space in between us to see if someone was after her because of me. I didn't agree but I had to do what was asked of me."

"I see." Detective Lee nodded. "You seem like a good guy, but this investigation just took a dark turn. Now that I have this added information, I can tell you that this case has gotten a lot more complicated. The thing is the nurse stated that the guy who brought Ms. Amora here claimed to be her boyfriend but couldn't answer any personal questions. He left right after being informed that the incident would have to be reported to the authorities.

Apparently, he was going to inform her family members. That was a red flag for the nurse as well. A boyfriend would know something. He didn't even know her birthday. According to the nurse, he only knew that Ms. Amora was from New Orleans, where she worked, and where she lived. Whoever this guy is isn't too bright. If we find him, I believe we'd find the person that's been stalking you and Ms. Amora. I'll try to get the surveillance footage from the entrance of the ER. Do you think she can spot the guy if she sees him?" I raised my arm as high as I could to get their attention.

"What's wrong baby girl?" Kris asked me. I got my notepad and wrote, "I WILL KNOW."

Detective Lee walked to the left side of my bed and reintroduced himself to me. "As you've heard, I'm trying to get some information about your assault. If you're willing to write you can write. If you can nod, you can do that as well. I don't want to cause you any more discomfort than you're already feeling. You understand?" I nodded. "Did you leave work at noon?" I nod. "Your sister stated that she spoke with your assistant. Do you by any chance have her number in your phone?" I nod. I wrote her name on my notepad, but Kristine beat me to it.

"Her name is Erica." Kristine said.

"I'd have to speak with her in order for us to back track your steps." I nodded. "Do you remember texting Mr. Noel before your assault took place?" I nodded. "Did you go into your home once you'd gotten there?" I shook my head. "So, whoever did this to you did this as you were exiting your vehicle?" I nodded. "Did you get a good look at the guy or woman?" I shook my head. "Did you see his face at all?" I shook my head. "Are you by any chance dating anyone else besides Mr. Noel?" I shook my head. I grabbed my pen and notepad. I wrote "Curtis." "You date a guy named Curtis?" Detective Lee asked me. I wrote, "I met" on my notepad. "Oh okay, you met a guy named Curtis?" I nodded. "When did you meet this guy, Curtis?" I wrote "today" on the notepad. "Does he work with you?" I shook my head. I wrote "the third floor" on my notepad. "He works on the third floor of your building?" I nodded. "Have you seen this guy in your building before today? I shook my head. "That's enough for now. I have a name and a location. I'll try to get some surveillance footage from here and from your office. Hopefully the next time you see me, I'll be letting you know that we caught the guy." He touched my hand, "Get some rest." he said as he headed towards the door. He shook Noel's hand. "You have a strong woman. You take care of her now. It was nice to meet the both of you." Detective Lee exited my room.

Chapter 18

Amora was being discharged after four days of being cooped up in her hospital room and one day after my birthday. I knew that she wasn't comfortable in the hospital bed, so I had our moms get Amora's condo nice and comfy for her. I rearranged my schedule so I could wait on her hand and foot. Her mom had flown in Tuesday morning and had been staying with Amora every day since. My mom and dad made it out here Tuesday afternoon. Ms. Ann, Amora's mom and my mom were getting along just fine. It was as if they had known each other all their lives.

Once I had made it to Amora's room with the wheelchair, she was sitting on the side of the bed with her phone in her hand. Then my watch played a tune. I read the message.

My Love: We need to talk ASAP!

"How you doing Ms. Ann? Was she a good patient for you today?"

"Hey handsome. I'm doing well now that my baby gets to go home. She was fine before that girl had come here to visit her."

"Girl?"

"Yes, a young lady. She said that her name was Tia or something like that. She told Amora that you had told her what happened and that she was here in the hospital. She brought her some flowers and a 'Get Well Soon' card. Amora was resting at first but had woken up just as Tia was leaving the room."

I looked to Amora for confirmation. I could see in her eyes that her mom was dead on with what she wanted to talk to me about. "I haven't spoken to Tia since the lunch we had. I haven't told her anything. I sure as hell didn't tell her about what happened to you." Tears started to fall from Amora's eyes. "Ms. Ann, can you give us a minute alone please?"

"Sure baby. I'll go chat with the nurse for a second."

"Thank you." I said as she walked out. I looked back at Amora and grabbed her hands. "Babe, I know that this is hard for you to process and it's hard for you to trust anyone right now but I need you to trust me. I have not told Tia anything. Maybe Noble told her that you were here. I'll call and speak with him as well. Something isn't adding up Amora and I'm going to get to the bottom of it by any means." I held her head up by her chin making her look into my eyes. "I love you Amora and I'm going to find the person that did this to you."

I transferred Amora from the bed to the wheelchair as I prepared to take her home. I put all of her flowers on the rolling cart that her nurse had given to me to help transport everything to the car. I put Amora's duffle bag on my shoulder and began to roll Amora out of the room. As I got closer to the nurse's station Ms. Ann assured me that she'd double check the room to make sure I didn't leave anything behind. I asked if she wanted me to wait for her, but she told me to get Amora to the car. I told her where the car was parked and continued to walk.

****

When we got to Amora's condo there were flowers everywhere. My mom and Kris did their best to make room for all of them but some of them had to be put outside. Mainly the potted ones. That worked out perfectly because Amora loved flowers. My mom also put all of the "Get Well" cards together for Amora to read as well.

I assisted Amora to the bathroom so that she could take a shower. The nurse said that it would help her with the pain and help her to relax. I grabbed one of my old button ups I left over and a pair of panties for Amora. I locked the door so no one would walk in on us in the shower. I removed my clothes first then Amora's. I helped her in the shower, being careful not to make her move her arms too much. The water was hot just the way Amora liked it. With her back to me, she let the shower run on her boobs. A soft moan came from her lips. I could tell that she was crying. I slowly began to wash her back.

Amora turns to face me. I felt so powerless because I couldn't take her pain away. I couldn't make her feel better. She lays her head on my chest as she continued to cry. I gently hug her around her waist, trying not to squeeze her too tightly. "It's going to be okay. You're safe now. I'm here to protect you. I will make sure that no one leaves you alone. We are all here to take care of you." I say trying to assure her the best way I could. I then wash Amora and myself. I get out of the shower first then I help Amora out. I dry her off and dress her. I wrap

145

the towel around my waist before helping Amora to her bed. She immediately motions for me to sit next to her.

"As much as I want to believe you had nothing to do with Tia coming to see me I can't. Not after the photo and hotel key, I can't.

"Amora, you know I couldn't stand that girl. Why would I even talk to her after what she pulled at Thanksgiving?"

"Well, you did see her AFTER Thanksgiving."

"Yes, I did. But that was because I thought she wanted to apologize for what she did."

"That still doesn't make it okay Noel. You didn't even ask me how I felt about it nor if I thought it was a good idea. Truth be told, she didn't just hurt you with what she said, she hurt me too. Why apologize to just you. What about me, your mom and Noble?"

"You're right. I didn't think to call you because you said you wanted nothing to do with me. Babe, I'm sorry I didn't give you a heads up. It will never happen again."

"I want to believe that I do but I can't. I need you to give me a day or two to figure this all out. You can stay the rest of the day, but I need some space."

"If space is what you need, I'll give you that but I'm not going anywhere tonight." Amora nods. "I'm going to call Detective Lee and tell him about Tia's visit. I told you something is strange about that." She nods again. I kiss her on her forehead and leave the room.

In the living room, Ms. Ann and Kris are deep in conversation, they don't even notice me walking in. I go into the fridge. "I already made Amora's smoothies for the day." My mom yells at me from the dining table. I grab a smoothie and head back to Amora's bedroom. I put the straw into the smoothie and put it to Amora's lips. She takes a small sip and shakes her head. "What's wrong?" I asked her. She said it had given her a brain freeze. "I'll let it sit for a few minutes." I sit the smoothie on her nightstand.

Now realizing that I'm still wearing just a towel I go to the drawer and grab a pair of boxers and a pair of shorts. I grab my phone from the dresser and call Detective Lee. He answers on the first ring. "Just the man that I wanted to speak with." He says as he answers the phone.

"Did you get any leads?"

"Unfortunately, no, I hit a bit of a snag. I went over to see Ms. Amora but they told me that she had been discharged."

"Yes, she was discharged this afternoon. We are with her at her condo. I wanted to speak with you about something though."

"What is it?"

"Amora's mom told me that my former sister in-law, Tia went to visit Amora this morning."

"Okay." He says as if trying to understand my point.

"The problem is that she told them I sent her to check on Amora. That's not true at all. I haven't spoken with Tia since the week after Thanksgiving. The hotel incident I told you about."

"I see. I see."

"What's the snag?"

"We went to Amora's office building, and no one knew a Curtis. I spoke with Ms. Erica also. She said that this Curtis guy called Amora Monday morning but couldn't remember the number he had called from. She said that he had been transferred to her line. We went through the surveillance that we received from the hospital, and we were able to capture a picture of the guy with Amora. It's not a good enough picture but I was thinking that she could possibly identify him if she saw him."

"Maybe so. Also Ms. Ann told me that Tia left a gift for Amora at the hospital. Would that be any help to you?"

"Do you think Tia is the one that hurt Amora?"

"There is no way to know for sure. I'm desperate. I just want to know who hurt her."

"I understand. I'll tell you what. Since Ms. Amora is just getting home, I'll give her a day to get comfortable before coming over. Also, if someone is watching her, they'll know that she has a lot of foot traffic coming through. I will come in an unmarked car at noon tomorrow. Does that sound like a plan?"

"Absolutely. I'll update our parents. Thank you, Detective."

"My pleasure. We will find the person behind hurting your fiancée."

"I sure hope so." I say as I end the call. I walk towards Amora, who's scanning me. "That was Detective Lee. He said that they were able to get a picture from the hospital footage. They'll come over tomorrow to see if you can identify the guy in the photo. You want some more smoothie?" She nods. I raise the bottle and puts her straw to her lips. I'm going to get a pair of gloves and go through those cards. If there are any prints on them, I don't want to get them smeared or something." I shrug. "You never know. I'm desperate. I need to know who did this. I want to kill them myself."

When Amora's done with her smoothie, I leave the bedroom to put the bottle in the sink. Afterwards I grab a pair of gloves from the drawer to go through the cards. "Who you about to perform surgery on?" Kris asks me from the couch. I chuckle. "I'm about to go through these cards to see if I can find something suspicious."

"That's a good idea son." My mom assures me. "Have you heard anything else from the detective?"

"I just spoke with him. He told me that he'll come over around noon tomorrow to show Amora a photo they retrieved from the hospital footage."

"How's Amora feeling about all of this?"

"Traumatized. I hate this for her, and I hate the person that did this to her."

"That's a strong word son." My mom says.

"And I mean it, Mom. He could've killed her." I felt myself becoming emotional. Just the thought of it upset me. Had I left soon as she texted me, I probably could've caught him. I would've beat him till his death. I want him dead. I want to be the one to kill him. He hurt the love of my life. He scarred my heart by doing what he did to Amora.

"I know you do baby boy but don't let him or anyone put hate in your heart. I raised you to love your sisters and brothers. I taught you to forgive those that needed it, not for them but for you." My mom rubs the side of my face with the back of her hand. She always knew how to calm me.

Ms. Ann chimes in, "Your mom is right Noel. As much as I want to hate the person that did this to my daughter, I can't bring myself to. All I want to know is why. Why her?"

"That's what I'm having a problem with. I can't accept any reason for why this was done to her. She didn't deserve this."

"This conversation is a little too deep and emotional for me. I need to step out for a minute. Noel let me know if you come across anything." Kris says as she walks into the bedroom with Amora.

I sit at the dining table to open the cards and read them. "Who has the initials P.P.E.?" I ask aloud to no one in particular. Both our moms were looking at me with a crazed expression. I put the card back into its proper envelope and sat it to the side. I made a mental note to ask Amora if she knew anyone with those initials. In her field of work PPE meant personal protective equipment. Was it supposed to be some sort of inside joke or something? I was going to ask her once I was done going through them all.

Chapter 19

Kris had come into my room just as I started dozing off. It was hard for me to fall asleep and stay asleep. I texted her and asked that she get me one of my pain pills. She did what I asked of her. She was worried and I could see it all in her face. I was tired of worrying and crying. I just wanted it all to be over. I wanted the detective to find the person that did this to me. He was out there. I felt like he was watching my every move. It made me feel uneasy.

My eyelids were getting heavy. I was dozing off again. I was on cloud nine. I was relaxed. I was floating. I didn't have a care in the world. Noel rushed into my bedroom. "Babe, do you know someone with the initials P.P.E.?" I frowned at him because not only was I trying to get some rest, but exactly what the fuck was he asking me? "I know what PPE means babe. Someone signed one of your cards PPE. I didn't know if it was some sort of inside joke or not." That was the last thing I heard come from Noel's lips, I was fast asleep.

When I woke up the house was quiet. Kris was no longer in the bed next to me. I reached for my phone on the nightstand. I texted Noel asking what he was doing and where he was. He shot me back a sarcastic text asking why it matters to me since I needed space. He had a valid point. I sat the phone back on the nightstand and got up to use the bathroom. It hurt a little when I pushed myself off the bed. On the way to the bathroom, I heard a noise come from the living room. I changed direction and headed towards the noise.

When I opened my bedroom door, I saw something that I had never wanted to see in my life. Tia was sitting on the couch with my mom and Kris. They were having a grand time talking and laughing. "What's she doing here I asked?"

"She came over to check on you and was giving me the scoop on Angie and Noel's brother." Kris says. "Do you need something? You hungry?"

"I was going to the bathroom but then I heard a noise. I came to see where it had come from. Kris, you know I don't like that hoe. Get her the fuck out of my house NOW!"

"You don't mean that. That's just the pain pills talking."

"Kris, I said what the fuck I said. You either put that hoe out or I'd put the both of you out."

They both laughed at me as if I said something funny. I wasn't in a laughing mood. I wanted the hoe out of my house. I couldn't stand her ass after what she had done at Noel's parents' house for Thanksgiving. She had to get the fuck out and fast before I lost my cool. "I have something that'll make her ass run out of here. Stay right there, Tia. I'll be right back." I walked into my bedroom to get my .380 from my underwear drawer. I got it after the mysterious envelope was delivered to me.

The hoe was bold because she walked into my bedroom not long after I did. "Amora why you acting like we're not sisters? We're dating brothers."

"Bitch if you don't get the fuck out of my house, I'll have your ass removed in a body bag." I said as I aimed my gun towards the middle of her forehead. I followed her as she hurriedly exited my bedroom. Back in the living room she was collecting her things. She tells Kris, "Your sister is fucking crazy. You can't be nice to some people. I'm about to go home to Noel. I'll have to talk to you later."

"What did you say bitch?" I shot her right there. Her body dropped in slow motion. I watched as a pool of blood formed around her head.

I I I I I I I I I

"Amora! Amora!" I heard Noel yelling my name. I opened my eyes to find myself sitting on the toilet. I looked up at him. "I told you to text me if you needed to use the bathroom. I'm happy I walked in here when I did. It's good to see you being mobile though. How's your pain? Is it still unbearable?" I nodded. He let me wipe myself then helped me back to my bed.

I picked up my phone from the nightstand. I had a bunch of 'get well soon' texts from a few my colleagues. Jake had told everybody what happened to me with my permission of course. He even gave Erica a few days off to cope. She came to visit me a couple of times while I was in the hospital. She told me to call her if I needed her no matter what it was I needed. Erica was good people. She was going to be my personal assistant when I went back to work. I was about to reply to some of the text until I noticed it was after 2am.

"I had a weird dream."

"About what?" He asked.

"Tia was here talking and laughing with my mom and Kris. She said she was going home to you, and I shot her."

"That was definitely a dream. Noel says with a chuckle. "No way in hell she's coming home to me, and I highly doubt Kris would let her inside of your house."

"I'm positive Kris wouldn't let her in here. There's nothing she can say to me after what she did. I wouldn't be surprised if she popped up over here trying to check on me. She did say something alarming in my dream though."

"What was that?"

"She said 'you can't be nice to some people'."

"That's true. Why was that so alarming?"

"That's same thing I told Curtis when he called me at work on Monday."

"Could be your woman's intuition trying to tell you something." Noel says. "Do you need anything before I head out?" I shake my head. "We have a busy day tomorrow, so I need you to be well rested. I'll be right here when you wake up in the morning. Your mom is in your office. The alarm is set, and Mel has a couple of her guys watching for anyone suspicious. Angie came over for a little while earlier, but you were knocked out." Noel kissed my forehead and I fell asleep.

The next morning my mom woke me up at 8am talking about it was time to eat and do my breathing exercises. I pointed to the bathroom to let her know that I needed to use the bathroom first. Noel came over to help me out of bed. After I was done using the bathroom, Noel rinsed my mouth out with the prescribed rinse that my doctor gave me. It was supposed to help with the healing of my gums. Then he washed my face with a warm towel.

I went out into the bedroom where my mom was still waiting for me with my smoothie and incentive spirometer in hand. I was not a fan of the breathing exercises because it would put too much pressure on my ribs and cause more pain than usual. My mom wasn't going to let me miss a beat. I was her baby girl. If she could've healed me herself, I would've been healed Tuesday morning when she arrived.

When I was done with my exercises, Noel helped me to the living room where everyone else was. Mrs. Betty was at the stove cooking breakfast for those that could eat it. Mr. Nathan was in front of the TV watching ESPN. How typical? Kris and my mom were prepping the table for everyone to eat. It was good to see my mom and Mrs. Betty getting along so well. The food smelled wonderful, but my smoothie had filled me up.

I responded to text messages while everyone ate their breakfast. It was hard not to do any work, but my doctor told me to give myself at least two weeks to rest. I was always working. I was working when I wasn't working. Erica had sent me a text telling me about her conversation with Detective Lee. In the text she apologized for not being of more help. I replied to her assuring her that she did the best she could do with the little information she did have. She was taking it hard also. She said that she should've talked me into staying at the office that day. She was feeling guilty, but I told her that I was grateful for her. I told her that everything was going to be okay even though I didn't really believe it myself. I fell asleep soon after.

Detective Lee and Detective Wilcox arrived at my house at about 11:30am. Noel welcomed them to have a seat on the couch. At this time, it was just my mom and Noel at the condo with me. Mr. and Mrs. Brown had left to do some shopping. Kris left for work but promised that she'd be back later.

"Good morning. It's good to see you on this side of the hospital Ms. Amora." I nodded. "Well, I'll get straight to it. I've spoken with every company within your building, and no one seemed to know a Curtis. I also spoke with Ms. Erica her information on Mr. Curtis was limited as well. What I told Mr. Noel on yesterday was that I needed you to take a look at this screenshot we were able to retrieve from the hospital footage. Let us know if the person looks familiar to you. The issue that remains though is we don't know if Curtis is this guy's real name or if he's using an alias."

Detective Wilcox goes into his briefcase and pulls out a manila folder. Inside of the folder were pictures of the crime scene along with a couple of screenshots. I let out a moan when my eyes fell on a screenshot of a guy carrying my lifeless body as Detective Wilcox placed it on the coffee table. I cried. My ribs hurt. My jaw hurt. The tears were falling uncontrollably. Noel tightened the grip he had on my hands.

"That's Curtis. That's him."

The detectives watch the interaction between Noel and me. "She said that's the guy. That's the Curtis guy." Noel tells the detectives.

"Are you sure that's the same guy?" Detective Lee asked me. I nodded.

"That's the same thing he was wearing Monday when I met him. He needs to get footage from the coffee shop. We were in the same line."

"Is there a way you can get the footage from the coffee shop? At least that would put him in the same place as her and a time frame." Noel stands up and walks over to the island. "Look at this card. I went through all of her 'Get Well Soon' cards last night. This one stood out because someone signed it PPE."

"Personal Protective Equipment?" Detective Wilcox said aloud.

"That's the same thing I was thinking when I saw it. In Amora's line of work, it's mandatory that they wear PPE. I didn't know if it was an inside joke or not." Noel said and then it hit me.

I stopped crying and tried to stand up. My mom rushed over to help me. "You have to take it easy Amora." She said in her mom voice.

I had everyone's attention at that point. "This beating was personal. On my first day at Sawyer Engineering Inc, I was scheduled to do a site visit. When I arrived there was a guy, I can't remember his face. He was flirting with me. I told him that I was there to see his boss's boss and was going to have him fired for using machinery without wearing the proper PPE."

I turned back to the coffee table and pointed to the pictures. My mom reached them to me. My heart dropped. It was coming back to me. Curtis was the guy I had gotten fired this entire time. Then, Tia's comment played again in my mind 'you can't be nice to some people.' *What have I done?* I thought to myself. "Maybe I deserved this. He was just being nice. He just thought I looked good. Friendly flirting. I was doing my job. Oh my God! He was talking about me when he said people let their jobs go to their head. He was referring to me." All I could do was cry.

Noel came and laid my head in his chest as I cried. My mom went to get my pain meds. Detective Lee removed the pictures from my hand and passed them to Detective Wilcox.

He put the pictures back into the folder and the folder back into his briefcase. "Ms. Amora you were only doing your job. Do not in any way allow yourself to feel guilty for this happening to you. The guy is scum. The bottom line is his ego was bruised the minute he realized you weren't moved by his flirting. You remained professional. His male chauvinistic attitude couldn't handle that. He needs to be held accountable for his actions. I'm going to take this card that Mr. Noel gave to me and have it dusted for prints. I pray that we find a match." Detective Lee said to me.

"I'm going to take a trip to the coffee shop myself and see what information they can help me with. Also, do you remember the contractor's name from that site? Detective Wilcox added.

"I can do you one better. I still have the superintendent's phone number. He asked that I kept him in the loop for future projects.

"You mind calling him for me?" Detective Wilcox asked. I shake my head. I dial his number after finding his contact. Detective Wilcox takes the phone and puts it on speaker.

"This is Chuck." He says as he answers.

"Good afternoon Mr. Chuck. My name is Detective Wilcox. Do you have a minute?

"Yes, I do."

"I'm calling you in reference to Ms. Scott. She's the project manager over at "

"Yeah, yeah. I know Ms. Scott. I thought this was her calling me."

"She did call you Sir. There's been an incident and we need a bit of information. I was hoping you could help with that."

"Sure. I'll most certainly try to help where Ms. Scott's concerned. What kind of incident if you don't mind me asking."

"I'm not allowed to say Sir. I'm sorry."

"Is she okay?" Chuck asks. Everyone looks at me. I nod my head.

"Uhh, yes Sir. She's doing as best she can do given the circumstances. Mr. Chuck, I need you to go back down memory lane for a second."

"I'll try."

"Ms. Scott said she made a visit to a site you were supervising. Can you recall that visit?"

"Uhh, yea. Yeah. She came maybe the middle of October."

"Do you remember what took place during that visit?"

"I surely do like it was yesterday. Ms. Amora wasn't pleased with the guys' work ethic. I ended up letting go one of my workers and my foreman that day." Detective Wilcox looks at me.

"Do you by any chance remember the worker's name? Was he a young guy?"

Mr. Chuck chuckles. "His name is uhh, Jacob. Jacob Macintyre. He was in his twenties I believe. Wait a minute. Did he do something to Ms. Scott? The guy took it really hard when I let him go. He started destroying supplies and swearing at some of the other guys and myself. I knew then that I had made the right choice by letting him go. The guy was nuts."

"Thank you for your time, Mr. Chuck."

"No problem. I'm happy to help."

Detective Wilcox ends the call and looks to me for confirmation.

"That sounds about right. When he called me at work, he mentioned something about people taking their jobs to their heads and power tripping. Besides Erica, he was the last person I spoke with before leaving work on Monday. Isn't this what you all call motive. I cost him his job by doing my job."

"You are absolutely correct Ms. Amora. He does have a motive and now we have a name. I appreciate your time. I'm going to head back to the headquarters with this new information and see what I can find. As always, call me if you need me. Hopefully I'll be calling you first." Detective Lee says before leaving.

Chapter 20

Norman called saying I was needed in the office; it was some type of emergency. He rarely called me about business. I knew it had to be something urgent. I got everything squared away with Ms. Ann and headed straight to the office. Amora had already fallen asleep, so she didn't know I left. I made a mental note to check on her once everything was sorted out with Norman. The entire ride to the office I contemplated what the situation could've been and who may have been involved.

When I pulled up to the office I spotted my dad's rental car in the parking lot. I even spotted Nathan's car which was strange considering the time of day it was. Nathan hated being in the office. It took too much time away from the ladies in his opinion. Maybe since he'd been involved with Kris, he'd turned a new leaf. Still, I shrugged it off and walked into the building.

"Good to see you big bro." Norman says as he reaches out to shake my hand.

"Same. What's the urgency?"

"You're probably going to want to sit down for this one."

"Sit down?" I frowned." Man, if you don't tell me what's going on " I took a seat

Nathan locks the entrance to keep the public from interrupting our family meeting or what I'm assuming to be a family meeting. My dad comes to stand on the right side of me and places his hand on my shoulder. "*Was this some kind of intervention?*" I thought to myself. For the life of me I couldn't understand why they were all here. What could it have been? I scanned my mom and dad for answers. Neither of them said a word. Instead, my dad tightened his grip on my shoulders.

Noble came from behind Norman. "Mom told me that Tia went to visit Amora in the hospital."

"She did. She told Amora's mom that I sent her there. Did you tell her what happened to Amora?"

"Hell no, I didn't tell her anything. I spoke with Tia to see if I could get some information out of her. She was acting nonchalant when I asked where she heard about what happened. I haven't been talking to her since the hotel stunt she pulled with you. Mom said that the detective was coming to meet with you two today."

"He did. We met with them this morning. What are you getting at though?"

"Well yesterday, Tia came to my crib talking about how much she missed me and wanted to see me."

"Okay and?"

"Hurry up and get to the point Noble. It seems like you're stalling." Nathan says in a big brother tone.

"I think Tia may have had something to do with Amora's attack."

I stood up from the chair. "What the hell do you mean Tia may have had something to do with it. She either did or she didn't. I told you to leave that crazy bitch alone when you met her. We all did. But no, you had to convince all of us of how good she was to you." I looked at my parents. "I'm sorry Mom." Then back at Noble, "You better find that trifling hoe before I do."

"Noel, can't you just tell the detective to question her or something?" Norman questions.

"No, it doesn't work like that. We don't have any evidence. We'd need something that could prove her to be a suspect or an accessory." I turned back to Noble. "What brought you to believe Tia had something to do with the assault?"

"Her phone rang, and she ran to the bathroom. She said she had to take the call privately. I didn't think anything of it at first but then I heard her yell, 'I wanted the bitch dead not in the fucking hospital!' I knocked on the bathroom door and asked her if everything was alright. Then, she walked out of the bathroom like nothing happened. I just felt like it was kinda odd that she was having a conversation about someone being in the hospital. The phone rang again, and I saw the name Jacob pop up on the screen. I don't know about you but that was one hell of a coincidence to me."

"It surely is considering we found out that the guy's name is Jacob just this morning. I'm about to contact the detective. He may ask you to go in for questioning. Track her phone and get her location."

"I already tried either she turned her location off or she's just not sharing it with me anymore."

"Great." I say with sarcasm. "Simply saying you saw the name in her phone doesn't hold any weight. I need something that puts her there." I turn to my mom. "Mom don't be surprised if they call you in for prints. Remember that weird card I found last night? I gave it to the detectives to dust for prints. Since you put all of the cards together your prints may be found. I hope Tia's prints are found as well. That'll be just what we need to put her as an accessory. Ms. Ann did tell you that Tia was the one brought the card, right?"

"Correct. She did." My mom said while nodding. "Noel baby, I need you to get yourself together before we let you go. Your dad and I only came to keep you levelheaded. We all know how you feel about Amora as well as Tia. I don't need you going out there doing something stupid that'll cause harm to you, your reputation or jeopardize your freedom. What good would you be to Amora then? *'Vengeance is mine, said the Lord.'* You remember that."

"I thought this was an intervention." I said with a chuckle.

"I wish that's what it was." Noble said with a deep sigh. "That would've been easier. You don't have any bad habits that I know of."

"Thanks for the compliment."

"Hey Mom, is it safe to unlock the door now?" Nathan asks.

"Yes sweetheart. I need to head back to Amora's to relieve Ann." She kisses us all on the cheek before leaving with our dad. I headed to my office to do a little paperwork.

"How are you really holding up?" Norman asked as he stuck his head in my doorway.

"You can come in you know." He does. "Truth is, I feel helpless. I want to help her and protect her, but I can't. Not without getting arrested anyway. It's frustrating to see her hurting like that. Witnessing the way, she broke down today when they showed her his picture did something to my heart. Man, I never want to be someone that hurts her like that." I said as I shook my head.

"You'd never be that person Noel. There are some evil people in the world whether we like it or not. You won't be able to save her from everything or everybody. You just have to hope for the best and pray as Mom would say."

"It's ironic that you said that because since Thanksgiving I've been trying to keep Tia away from Amora. All along this guy has been stalking her since her first day of work. Turns out he did this to Amora because she got him fired. Fact of the matter is, he got himself fired. She reported him to his boss for not following policy. She was doing her job. He shouldn't be angry with anyone but himself. Amora didn't deserve what he did to her."

"I agree. There's nothing a woman could do to me that'll make me assault her that way. She's a female. Just knowing her in this short period of time I know that she's without malice."

"Right! She's resilient though."

"Well, you know we have your back if you need us. Don't hesitate to call us." Norman says as he gets up from his seat.

"I'm good. I'm about to finish up this last file then head back to Amora's." We dapped and Norman went on his way.

When I was done, I called Ms. Ann to check on Amora. She said that she was still napping and asked that I stop to pick up a few things. Amora was running low on ice cream and strawberries for her smoothies. Her appetite had started to pick up since she had been home. What she didn't know was that I would've done anything for Amora. I wanted to give her the world.

Chapter 21

It was a few days after meeting with Detective Lee before we'd gotten any updates. He spoke with my mom when he called, letting her know that Curtis, well Jacob, had prior convictions and was found in their database. He told her that he needed me to look at a full lineup to make everything official. I told my mom that I was willing. That man had broken my jaw and ribs. He made me afraid to sleep in my own house. He'd beat me so badly that I could've died. If the detectives needed me to point him out a million times I would've did it every time. I wanted him arrested ASAP.

Detective Wilcox came straight over with the photo lineup. I pointed Curtis out soon as I laid eyes on his photo. He looked scary on his photo, but I could still tell that it was him by his eyes. I'd never forget his eyes. Detective Wilcox told me to write my initials on the photo and to sign the back of the page. I did as I was told. He explained to me the next steps were to get with North Texas Crime Commission to get help from the citizens of Dallas. He told me that Jacob would probably hide out after the news break of him being primary suspect in my assault.

"My best advice to you is to be aware of your surroundings at all times. Keep your alarm set. Try not to be left alone for long periods of time. Most of all DO NOT contact him in any way."

"We don't leave her home alone at all." My mom says. "I do have a question though."

"Shoot." Said Detective Wilcox.

"What did you all find from the envelope my son in law gave to you during our last meeting?"

He sighs. "Well, we submitted it for processing. The lab tech is trying to retrieve a salvia sample from the seal. That can take anywhere from a week or two. We're hoping to hear something sooner than later."

"Hopefully." My moms and I nod.

The detective stood to leave. "I don't want to hold you too much longer. I have to get back to headquarters. Detective Lee and I will do the best we can to get you justice Ms. Amora. You ladies enjoy the rest of your day."

As Detective Wilcox is leaving Mrs. Betty and Mr. Nathan are walking in. My Ring sent a notification to my phone. From the number of bags, they were carrying I assumed Mrs. Betty and my mom planned to have Christmas at my house. I was inconveniencing everyone around me. They all had to change their plans to babysit me. I was getting bothered by that. The only person that hadn't been around was Noel. He was giving me the break that I asked for but didn't really want. I texted hm.

Mr. Nathan turned the television on the news as soon as he sat on the couch. I was mid text when I heard the news reporter say, "If you know the whereabouts of Mr. Jacob Macintyre, please call North Texas Crimestoppers at 214-373-TIPS. There is a $5000 reward for his arrest." I looked around and all eyes were on me. I collected my things and walked to my bedroom. I didn't want them to see my tears.

Noel responded to me letting me know that he was doing a business deal and that he'd have to talk with me later. My feelings were a little hurt. I responded with a sad face. I finished my smoothie and pulled out my laptop. I started to do all the research that I could on Jacob Macintyre. When his mug shot popped up, I began to cry and closed my laptop. I texted Noel again.

Me: I want you here.

My Man: I'll be there in the next thirty minutes or so. What's wrong? Do you need anything?

Me: Just you.

My Man: I'll be there to hold you in a little bit. I have to finish up this meeting first. I'll try to hurry up.

Me: Kk.

I took some pain meds and fell asleep.

Noel woke me up with a kiss on my lips. He was a freak, so he'd always peck first then lick my lips. I loved it when he did it too. He told me that he was about to take a shower, but he wanted to let me know that he'd made it. *"Oh, how sweet of him waking me up when I could've slept another thirty minutes,"* I think sarcastically. I checked my phone and saw that it was after 8pm. I started my nap a little after the 5 o' clock news. He told me that he'd be here in thirty minutes. That was over two hours ago.

I got out of the bed and walked into the bathroom. Noel was undressing. I tapped him on his back. "What's up Babe?" He asked me without turning around. I tapped him again because what did he expect me to say behind his back. When he turned to face me, I tapped my watch. He caught where I was going rather quickly. "I was going to come talk to you after my shower. Get in here with me?" I shake my head. "Come on babe. Get in with me." I shake my head again. I pointed to the bed. "We can go there later but I want you in here with me now." He says as he starts reaching for my shirt.

He undresses me and I join him in the shower. The water felt so good on my back. Noel just hugged me as we stood in the shower. Then he started talking. "It's been a while since we've been alone. I just needed a minute with you alone. I was thinking about booking your mom a room so we could have the condo to ourselves for a couple of days. I didn't want to leave her here alone given the circumstances and my house is too far. Since none of that is a good idea, I decided to just make the best of it." I raised my head to kiss him on the cheek. He was always so sweet and thoughtful. "We closed a deal today baby. We took over Schmidt Inc." I gave him a high five. I know it pained him that he couldn't see my smile and I hated that for him. "That's why I was late getting in. The guys wanted to go to the bar to celebrate. With everything going on I couldn't pass up the invitation to a drink. I'm stressed babe."

The only sound you could hear was the water running. Noel had fallen silent. I couldn't tell if he was crying or not, but I know I was. I knew he was stressed. We all were. What was even more stressful was that I couldn't really express myself to him. I wanted to be heard. I needed to be heard. The pain in my ribs was getting more bearable but I still couldn't speak too much. I couldn't wait for the new year to have these wires removed.

After the shower Noel wrapped me up in a towel. I walked to lock my bedroom door and climbed into the bed. Noel climbed in and got on top of me. He kissed my lips. Then he went down to my breast and kissed me there too. He licked my nipples and nibbled on them one by one. I pulled him up to me and looked him in his eyes. He kissed my nose. I pushed his erection into my already wet pussy. We both moaned. It had been weeks since Noel had been inside of me. I knew that he was trying to be patient. I also knew that's why he had been so stressed. My man was missing me. Noel moved in and out slowly while he licked and sucked my neck. He was trying to make me cum, I know he was. I wasn't ready too. I wanted him just as bad as he wanted me. We grinded and moaned. Moaned and grinded. "I want you to come for me babe. Wet my dick up." He whispered in my ear. Noel licked my lips; just like that I came quick and hard. It made my face and ribs hurt. Noel started to go in full throttle as he thrusted harder into me. "I'm cummin. Fuck!" He slammed into me one last time before rolling over.

"That was so good Noel. Baby I miss you. I miss us."

"I told you; it's been a while. I've been wanting to make love to you since you texted telling me we needed to talk. My world stops when I'm inside of you."

"Aww babe, I'm sorry." I began to cry. I felt helpless. I wasn't the woman he needed me to be in that moment.

Noel lifted my chin with his hand. "Do not feel sorry for me. You didn't do this to yourself. This, what we're feeling is only temporary Amora. Do you hear what I'm saying to you?" I nodded.

"Detective Wilcox said that they may not be able to get a sample from that envelope for about a week or two. Hopefully sooner. They put Jacob on the news asking the citizens to call Crimestoppers. Everybody looked at me. I just got up and walked out. I'm tired of everybody being here. I feel like I'm a burden. I can do for myself. I'm not handicapped. You know I appreciate everybody being here but..."

"That's not too bad. I just hope that they can get one. As for as you being a burden, that's not true. All of these people are here because they love you. If they had somewhere else more important to be they'd be there Amora. I do understand how and why you feel the way you do but baby stop beating yourself up. Just focus on your healing. Physically, mentally, emotionally, and spiritually. Be patient with yourself. Give yourself some grace.

My mom knocked on the door. "Amora it's time for your meds and your smoothie." Noel gets out of bed, puts on his robe, and opens the door.

"Thank you, Ms. Ann."

"I'm sorry for interrupting ya'll time. I was getting ready to head to my room, but I didn't want Amora to miss her last dose." She walks over and gives me a kiss on the forehead. "Goodnight."

"Goodnight." Noel says as he closes the door behind her. He takes his robe off and gets back into bed with me. I drink my smoothie. Not long after I'm fast asleep.

Chapter 22

Christmas morning Noble called me frantic. All I heard was him yelling into the phone. I couldn't make out what he was trying to say. "Noble calm down and tell me what's going on."

"The fucking cops are here going through my shit. They said something about my address being the last known address for Jacob. I don't even know who the fuck that is. I'm losing my shit Noel. This gotta be some shit Tia put them up to."

"I'm on my way. I'm walking to my car now. Who's in charge?"

"Some nigga that said his name is Detective Wilcox."

"Calm down Noble. Let me speak with the detective. Noble let the people do their job. Don't argue with the police Noble."

"You sound like Dad. It's fucking Christmas!" Noble says then he's quiet.

"This is Detective Wilcox."

"Good morning, Detective. This is Noel Brown. I believe you're working the assault case for my fiancée, Amora."

"Yes Sir, Mr. Brown."

"The house you're searching is my brother's house. I'm sure he's already yelled that to you a couple of times."

He chuckles. "Yes, he did Sir. He's a hot head for sure. We're just following protocol."

"I'm on my way there now. I'm about ten minutes out. Can you tell me what's going on now?

"Well, as you know we've been following our leads to try solving the case for Ms. Amora's assault. Upon searching Mr. Jacob, your brother's address came up as Mr. Jacob's last known address. It'll be better if we continue this conversation when you get here Mr. Brown. Your mom and Dad are arriving now. I'm sure they'll have some questions for me."

"Sounds great. See you soon." I end the call and call our lawyer. I told him what's going on and where he could meet us if needed. Noble lived about thirty minutes away from Amora. When he called, I'd just happened to be making last minute runs for Ms. Ann and my mom.

All of my brothers were standing outside with our parents when I pulled up. I got out of my car and walked straight to Noble's front door. I could see that some of the S.W.A.T team had begun to clear out. I asked for Detective Wilcox. "We meet again." I said as I reached out to shake his hand.

"I apologize for the inconvenience, but we were doing our jobs."

"Oh, I understand. After he calms down," I turn to nod in my brother's direction, "I'm sure he will too."

"Guys we can wrap it up. Go spend Christmas with your families. Good work today." Detective Wilcox said to the last of the S.W.A.T members that were leaving."

"It was something I wanted to speak with you about."

"Sure, I have a minute."

"Amora told me that it'll take a week or two to get a saliva sample from that envelope I gave to you."

"Yes. I'm hoping to hear back any moment now with the results."

"I think I can help you. Remember the sister-in-law I spoke about?" He nods. "Well, Noble is the brother she was with. He told me a while back that she had come over to visit him and a guy named Jacob called her phone. He said he didn't think anything of it until he heard Tia yelling something about wanting her dead, not in the hospital. I texted the info to Detective Lee, but he hasn't responded yet. I didn't think it would hold any weight to be honest."

"I understand."

"But it's all making sense now. The card I gave you was brought to the hospital by Tia, my ex-sister-in-law. She used to live here with my brother. That phone call couldn't have been a coincidence. She must know something."

"I see. What's Ms. Tia's last name? I'll run her through the database and see what I can find out."

"Caston. Tia Caston."

"Got it. If you hear anything else no matter what it is, let myself or Detective Lee know. Any leads are better than no leads. We're here to help you. I appreciate your corporation."

"Absolutely. We need to find this guy."

"Might have to find you a spot on the force." He said with a chuckle.

"I'll think about it." I chuckled. We began to walk toward our cars. Detective Wilcox stops in front of Noble to shake his hand and apologize to him once again before heading out. I hug my mom and shake hands with my dad. Norman and Nathan are both leaning up against Noble's car. They're heated.

"This is messed up Noel. It's Christmas bro." Noble says.

"What were you two talking about?" My mom asked in a concerned tone.

"I told him about what happened the last time Tia came over to see Noble. I told him that she was the person that brought that card to the hospital." I sigh. "They better get ahold of her before I do."

"Don't you go talking that nonsense son. Let the police do their jobs. They're doing a hell of a good one too." My dad said.

"I don't think we should bring this to Amora right now. This won't do anything but make her feel worst." Said Nathan. "She's going to have a whole lot to say once they take those wires off."

"Tia better hope they catch her before then." Norman said jokingly. "I've saw Amora kickbox at the gym before."

I frown. "I told her to stop doing that. It's dangerous."

"It's a form of self-defense. Stop trying to be everybody's Superman." Noble says with a grin on his face.

"Were ya'll heading over to Amora's now or later?" I ask to no one in particular.

"I'll be there in about an hour or so. I'm gonna go see what damage they did to my crib. Save me some pie." Noble says before he daps me and heads for his house. Everyone else just got in their cars and headed to Amora's condo.

Chapter 23

I knew something was off when everyone arrived except Noble. It was normal for him to be late when Tia was with him. I was hoping he hadn't got back with her after what she tried to do. I sure hoped he knew better than to invite her to my house. Then again that's probably why he wasn't there. He knew she wasn't welcome.

Angie was the first to show up out of the girls. Kris had flown back to New Orleans to spend Christmas with her family. She assured me that she'd be back to bring in the new year with me. Melanie and Macey showed up about an hour later. Mel brought some wine, but I couldn't drink any of it because of the meds I was taking. I wasn't trying to risk it. My smoothies were just fine.

Mrs. Betty and my mom were warming the last of the food while Mr. Nathan set the table for everyone to eat. Those that couldn't fit in the dining area grabbed a spot on the couch to eat. Mostly the guys because they wanted to watch the game. My mom served me my smoothie first. She asked if I was okay with all of the different aromas floating around. I pointed to my room asking if she wanted me to go into my room. "No baby, I'm just asking if it's bothering you." She leans in closer to whisper in my ear. "I put some food and pie in the deep freezer for you to have once they take those wires off of your teeth."

I sat in my recliner as everybody ate and talked. It was a little depressing because I couldn't laugh at any of the jokes. Noel came to sit in the recliner with me after he finished eating. He said that he had some good news for me. "Oh, really? Like what?"

"I had a talk with Detective Wilcox earlier this afternoon. He said that he was going to investigate Tia and see what he could come up with. I told him that I think she had something to do with what happened to you."

"How would she?"

"I just feel like she does. She brought a card to the hospital that was signed 'PPE.' And Noble said one day she was at the house with him some guy named Jacob called her phone."

"I'm not sure who brought the card though. All of the cards were mixed up. And maybe she knows someone named Jacob as well."

"Babe she was arguing about you being in the hospital instead of being dead." The expression on Noel's face confirmed everything I had been feeling since the assault. Jacob was hoping I'd die when he brought me into the hospital. That's why he left. He had to leave in case I did. It was all making sense. My head began to spin. I felt dizzy. I tried to stand but I couldn't, my legs were weak. "Where you going babe?" Noel asked. I weakly pointed to my room. I was nauseated. I grabbed my head and rubbed my temples hoping that it would suffice, it didn't. I puked.

"Noel what's wrong with her? What happened?" I could hear my mom asking.

"I don't know. I was just talking to her."

"About what nigga? You made the girl pass out." Nathan said trying to be funny.

"Nathan, hush your mouth and help your brother get her to the bed." Mrs. Betty said. "We have to cut the wires, she's puking."

I heard everyone talking all at once, but I couldn't open my eyes. My head was pounding, Noel had to be the one carrying me because I smelled his Jimmie Choo Cologne. He brought me to the bathroom and rinsed my mouth. Someone put a towel on the back of my neck. The spinning began to subside. I was coming through. "Amora baby, are you okay? Do you think you need to go to the hospital?" My mom's nerves were worse than mine. I shook my head. "Do you want to take your medicine now?" I nodded. My mom made my medicine cocktail and within minutes I was out like a light.

Later that night when I woke up only Noble and Noel were in the living room. They looked to be deep in conversation when I walked into the living room. I pointed towards my mom's room and Noel told me that she had been asleep. I was turning to walk back into my bedroom when Noble said, "Amora I need to talk to you about something."

I threw my hand up as if to say, "what now?"

"I know the feeling trust me."

Noel helps me take a seat on the couch. I look at Noble and point to my ear. "Well, first I want to apologize again for Tia's actions. I had no idea the girl was so stupid and foolish." Noel and I look at each other. I wave my hand letting him know to keep going. "I don't know if Noel told you or not, but the police came to search my house earlier today looking for that Jacob dude. They claimed that my address was his last known address. I feel like Tia's trying to sabotage us. I had new locks installed which is why I was late coming over. I tried tracking her phone but she's no longer sharing her location with me. Noel's already spoken with the detectives, and we gave them Tia's information. I just thought that you should know."

I shrug. "Apology accepted. I knew something was off about her when I met her. The bitch is ignorant as fuck." They both chuckled. Noel didn't tell me anything about your house being searched."

"We didn't think it was appropriate to tell you about the search considering it was Christmas and we didn't know what state of mind you may have been in." Noble says to cover his brother's ass.

"It's getting crazier every day. Noel said that Jacob called Tia one day you were together. They know each other in some kind of way. Maybe they're in a relationship. Tia knows too much. The photos were of Noel and Tia. Maybe Jacob took them. Maybe they're working together to take me down. She wants Noel and I'm in her way. I'm the common enemy.

"That could be true but why involve me?" Noble asked.

"Tia could just be using you as a distraction. Giving your address to throw the detectives off. They have no address. They don't know where to look. We seem to be the only people coming forth that knows them. How long have you known Tia?"

"About six months." Noble says. I frown.

"You put up with that for six months? Whew chile. Sex must've been amazing." I say as I rolled my eyes.

"Nah, don't do me that. She seemed like good people at first. She was more reserved."

"I find that hard to believe." Noel says as he scratches his head.

"I'm not trying to be funny but I'm going to call a spade a spade. She saw you and saw money. She knew that coming on to you acting ratchet wasn't going to get you. Tia's not obtuse. She's just ignorant."

"I agree," said Noel.

"Alright bro. I get it. You don't have to lecture me. I can't read women like you do. All of the good ones always flock to you and Nathan anyway. I always have to get whoever's left over."

"Amora has single friends." I shot Noel a look. "Babe, come on. Noble and Macey would be good for each other." He says with a chuckle.

"Macey would run circles around Noble and you know it. Noble NO! She's not the one you'd want to bring home to Mrs. Betty. But considering you brought Tia home; it could possibly work. Anyway, I'm about to go to bed. I have a long day of smoothies and meds tomorrow."

The guys chuckle at my joke. Noel then follows me into the bedroom to help me get into bed. He kisses me on my forehead. "I'll be back after I put him out." Noel says. I didn't wait up, I went straight to sleep.

Chapter 24

It was New Year's Eve, and I was helping Nathan get his house together for the big party he was throwing later. The theme of the party was *"Moment for Life."* Nathan told me that Kris was the one that actually came up with the theme. It wasn't bad but I knew it wasn't Nathan's idea. He would've said something like "Pimps N Hoes" or "New Year, New Bitches." Yeah, Nathan was very ignorant.

Amora was still in bed when I called her. She had been getting more and more agitated because the detectives still hadn't found Jacob and Tia. We were about to go into the new year without her case being solved. I told her that I wanted her to join me at the party and she agreed. I was hoping that getting out of the house and letting her hair down would loosen her up a bit. She had been so tense. Ms. Ann was still visiting with us. My mom and dad were leaving the day after New Year's, so I think that's what made Amora decide to join me.

Norman was the chef as always. He had the kitchen set up like a buffet. It looked really nice and sophisticated. Norman was the go-to for catered meetings and parties. The boy had a gift, and we took advantage of it as much as he allowed us. Our mom helped Angie with a few of the table decorations. Kris wanted each table to have a floating candle centerpiece. The rest of us helped Nathan move the furniture around. We moved the sectional into the man cave so we could set up more tables in the living and dining areas. In total there were going to be four regular round tables and six bar-height pub tables. Kris was bringing in the new year with a bang.

We finished setting up everything a little after 6pm. I headed back to get Amora and Ms. Ann. She told me that she'd be dressed by the time I got there but had no idea what she was going to wear. I told her that it was going to be 8° by midnight. I have no idea why I did that because New Orleans never had temperatures like these. It got cold in Dallas. I remembered I had forgotten something at home, so I stopped at home before getting on the interstate.

The ride to Amora's felt like it was taking forever. Even with my music on I was agitated. I was anxious. I knew she wasn't going to be dressed and I still needed to get dressed. I needed to shower. The clothes I had on were a little dirty from all of the moving we did earlier in the day. Amora texted me.

My Love: How about I just wait till you get here and we take a shower together?

Me: Sounds like a plan. I need to shower anyway.

Me: I hope you weren't going to be dressed when I got there.

My Love: It's just so comfortable in my bed. It's all warm and toasty. The only thing missing is you.

Me: Aww. I miss you too Babe.

My love: How much longer are you gonna be? I think my mom is dressed already.

Me: I'm about twenty minutes out. Did you find what you're going to wear?

My Love: I'm sure I can find something in all of the clothes I've ordered.

Me: Start looking. You should have something by the time I get there.

My Love: Yes Sir.

I pulled into the driveway just before 7:30. I took my garment bag from the hook, grabbed my duffle bag off of the floor in the backseat, and headed to the door. I rang the bell so that Amora could see it was me at the door before using my key to get in. My baby was becoming more and more paranoid. "Hello Ms. Ann. How you feeling today?" I asked as I walked into the condo.

"Hey baby. I'm feeling much better now that you're here. That child of mine is so stubborn. She wouldn't get dressed because you weren't here. I told her that I'd help her. She shook her head and folded her arms." Ms. Ann throws her arms up. "You created that monster. You got my baby spoiled."

"You're right. I may have had a hand in her being spoiled but you had her for thirty-two years before me." We both chuckle. I kiss her cheek and head for Amora's bedroom.

Amora is still in bed when I walk into the bedroom. I just shake my head. She slides out of bed and walks past me. I noticed she was locking the door. My hands were full, but I could've locked the door. She then takes my garment bag and lays it across the foot of her bed. She takes my hand and walks to the bed. "Babe, I need to take a shower first. You know you don't like people in your bed dirty." She tugs at my shirt, so I pull it off.

Before I knew it, Amora was on top of me. My dick was harder than a cinder block. I watched as she slid my dick into her pussy. I closed my eyes as I took in the feeling. She was so wet and tight. Her pussy was warm. "I can get on top if it hurts you too much." She shakes her head. Amora rode my dick real slow. She whined and rolled her hips. She bounced. With each bounce her pussy opened up a little. The shit felt sensational.

When I felt myself about to bust, I turned Amora over on her back. It was my turn to take control. I licked and sucked her nipples. I played with her pussy and watched as she squirmed in the bed. I licked her clit until she came. I swallowed her nectar. I wiped my face then climbed on top. I eased my dick into Amora's pussy all the while going deep. It didn't take long for her to put her nails in my back. I pushed harder. I moved faster. With every thrust I went deeper. I kissed her lips, her cheek. I sucked her neck. "I want you to come for me one more time." I whisper into her ear. Her body started to shake underneath me. I slowed down my stroke. "Fuck!" I was about to cum. I stroked harder and faster. Faster and harder. I went deeper and deeper. Amora's moans grow louder and louder. I come.

I walked into the bathroom to turn the shower on. Amora stayed behind to remove the sheets from the bed. She joins me after she's done. To my surprise she doesn't adjust the water temperature when she gets in the shower. She washes and gets right out. I followed suit. However, I let the water run on my back a few minutes before getting out of the shower. The spot where Amora scratched me stung a bit when the soap came into contact with it.

Amora spent about twenty minutes trying to decide what to wear before getting dressed. It didn't take me long to get dressed. All of my clothes were prepped and ironed days ago. When I was done Ms. Ann and I sat in the living room talking. We talked until Amora was finished getting dressed. I guess she had to make sure her outfit was perfect.

Chapter 25

When Noel presented this New Year's Eve party to me, I was excited on the inside. I hadn't been outside of my home in weeks. My ribs were healing nicely from what my doctor said at my last appointment. I only had to wear the wires on my teeth for two more weeks. I told my mom that I wasn't going to take my meds because I wanted to celebrate with a glass of wine. I was blessed and I had so much to be thankful for.

Kris told me that the theme of the party was '*Moment for Life,*' so I had to think hard about what to wear. I had been buying clothes online left and right. A little retail therapy on my depressed days. It wasn't like I was wearing any of the clothes to work or anything. I'd just open the packages and hang the clothes up. I left the shoes in their boxes. I wasn't going anywhere.

Noel texted me telling me that he needed me to be ready when he got to my house, but he knew me better than that. It took me time to get ready, especially in the physical condition I was in. My mom offered to help but I didn't want my momma to see me naked. I'm a grown ass woman. I laid in bed until he got here. Then I gave him a lil treat to make him forget about me not being ready. He didn't have any complaints either.

It was freezing out, so I decided on a pair of blue high-rise jeans by 7 For All Mankind. Underneath my jeans I wore a pair of thermals to help keep my legs warm. For my top I wore a beige and black rolled-neck geometric sweater by Ralph Lauren. To keep warm, I wore my black wool peacoat by Mackage. I put on a cute pair of socks and covered them with a pair of black saddle leather knee-high boots by Burberry. I brushed my hair down and covered my head with my black Ralph Lauren beanie and grabbed my black Ralph Lauren mini 888 crossbody. By the time I was ready to walk out of my bedroom Noel peeked in to see what was taking me so long. I gave him my purses so he could switch them out for me while I put on my diamond stubs that I ordered from Tiffany's.

Once we were all in Noel's car, he brought it to my attention that it was 8:47pm. I just looked at him and rolled my eyes. He got to my house well after 7pm and we made love before we even started getting dressed. He was so annoying.

Why are men like this? He didn't have to point out the time to me. I could've stayed in my bed. Nathan lived an hour away, so a nap was certainly in store for me. My mom was excited to get out of the house just as much as I was. I knew she was going to talk to Noel the entire ride. I could hear her now. What's this area of Dallas called? What kind of food did your brother cook for the party? Will there be any single men at the party? Yea, he could deal with that on his own.

I woke up when I felt the car stop. There were a lot of people talking. Partying. Noel came to open the door for my mom and me. It was freezing. I had never felt cold weather like this in all of my life. I used to travel with my mom when I was younger, but we always traveled when it was warm out. We walked to Nathan's door and Kris was already standing there with the door open. "Get ready to have this '*Moment For Life.*' She said as she greeted us.

Mrs. Betty and Mr. Nathan were the next to greet me in the foyer. Mrs. Betty hugged me and expressed how excited she was to see me finally getting out of the house. Noel then took my hand and guided me into the living room. All of my girls were there. Mel, Angie, Macey and most importantly Kris. She kept her word when she said she'd be back for New Year's.

Nathan's house looked like a winter wonderland. There was faux snow on the floors throughout the house. The tables were covered with either white linen or silver sequin. There was also a balloon arch made with white, light blue and silver balloons. The treat table was full of goodies, cake pops, pretzel sticks, light blue and white gumballs, cookies shaped like snowflakes. It was extravagant. The buffet was set up so elegantly. There were light blue dry ice drinks. Multiple charcuterie boards with different types of snacks. They were also themed with the winter wonderland décor.

Noman had cooked everything from fried chicken wings to lamb chops. They really out did themselves. A New Year's party must've been a big thing for them since fireworks were illegal here in Dallas. All we did back in New Orleans was eat cabbage, black-eyed peas with cornbread and pop fireworks.

Kris walks up from behind me and says, "It's beautiful, isn't it?" Referring to the decorations I assumed. I nod my head. She turns me around and hugs me tightly. Before letting me go she kisses my cheek. "I love you sis. I'm so happy you came." It made me get a little emotional and I started to cry. Kris had been my best friend since we were eight years old. We had been through a lot growing up. Her 'I love you' always hit me differently. My mom handed me a paper towel to dry my eyes. I didn't realize we were being watched by the others.

"Amora." I hear Noel say. I turn around only to find him down on one knee. I was so in shock, I just stared at him as tears fell from my eyes. Noel takes my hands into his. "Babe since the moment I met you, I knew that I wanted to be with you for the rest of my life. It was God Himself that brought you here to Dallas just for me. I've loved you since the first time I laid my eyes on you. I love everything about you. I love being with you. I love being around you. I love looking at you. I just love you. I never want to imagine what my life would be like without you. Will you marry me?"

"Yes, I will!" I try to smile but it hurt a little. I nod so hard and fast that it gave a headache. Noel slides the ring on my finger before he stands to kiss me. He kisses me on my lips and hugs me tighter than he's ever hugged me. I groan in pain. This man loved me, and he was all mine. I loved Noel almost as much as I loved myself. He was truly an amazing man with a beautiful heart. He hugs and rocks for a few minutes. After Noel let me go, everyone came in for hugs and to give their congrats.

Kris got on the mic to give a speech. "Congratulations to Amora and Noel on your engagement." Everyone applauds. "Amora you are beautiful honey. You are resilient. You are courageous and most of all you're my sister. Once I got wind of what Noel wanted to do, I begged Nathan to let me make this night extra special just for you. I needed it to be perfect. We all pitched in to make this your 'Moment For Life'. I love you, Mo." Teary eyed I blew Kris a kiss. The party started.

"TEN, NINE, EIGHT, SEVEN, SIX, FIVE, FOUR, THREE, TWO, ONE. HAPPY NEW YEAR!" Everyone yelled but me. We all walked around the room giving everyone their first kiss and hug in the new year. Noel hugged and kissed me. "I wanted to bring this new year in with you being my fiancée officially." He says with a chuckle. "You've made me the happiest man alive Amora."

"Aww babe. I love you too. You're so sweet babe."

"I wish I could kiss you the way I want to kiss you."

"The doctor said I can get these wires off in two weeks. I can't wait either."

"How does it feel?"

"It hurts a little but you're worth a little pain. I'll rest when the night is over."

"I heard that." He says as he hugs me and rocks me to the rhythm of the music.

Noel and I left for his house a little after 3am. I was tired and I needed to take something for my headache. I spent all night talking to Noel and I was paying for it. My mom stayed at Nathan's with Kris. She said that she was going to let us newly engaged people have the house to ourselves for the night. I was sure that Noel was going to enjoy our time alone. He'd been trying to get us alone for some time now.

Chapter 26

When I woke up Noel wasn't in the bed. I slid out of bed and walked to the living room. Noel was sitting on the couch. It looked like he was deep in thought. I walked closer to him so he could hear me call his name. "Babe?"

He jumped. "Don't be sneaking up on me like that." He chuckled.

"Something wrong?"

"No. I was just daydreaming." I sat down next to him on the couch. "How you feeling?"

"I feel okay."

"Last night was fun. Watching you interact with the family was pretty cool too." Noel said to me.

"I had so much fun. Your cousins were nice. I didn't know what to expect at first. I surely wasn't expecting this." I say wiggling my left hand.

"I wanted to do it for Christmas, but you saw how that day went." He says with sarcasm written all over his face. I forgot to tell you to read it."

I slide the ring off. "Read it?"

"Y'ea, I had it engraved."

"My Amora Forever. Forever My Love." I read aloud."

"It's a 2.25 CTTW certified cushion-cut diamond in 14k white gold. It's almost as beautiful as you. When I saw this ring, I knew right then that I was going to propose to you at Christmas dinner. That was until Christmas morning was shot to hell." Noel slides the ring back onto my finger.

"I love it. I love you." I caress Noel's face and kiss him on the lips.

"I love you too." Noel stands up and reaches for my hand. I placed my left hand into his hand to show off my ring. He then leads me back to the bedroom.

Noel hugs me from behind as he kisses my neck and nibbles on my earlobe. I let out a light moan. My pussy became wet immediately. I closed my eyes as I took in the moment. I was ready, had been ready since Noel put the ring on my finger the first time. He turned me around and kissed my lips. He sucked my lips, then he bit my bottom lip gently. It turned me on. My blood was rushing through my body. My yoni was throbbing. My legs got weak.

I backed up to the bed signaling Noel that I was ready for him to make love to me. He helped me into the bed. With my legs hanging to the side of the bed, Noel slowly removed my panties. He caressed and kissed both legs as he slid my panties off. Once he had got them all the way off, he laid me back onto the bed. He started to slowly massage my pussy before sliding a finger inside, then two. He tickled my pearl, and it sent me through a whirlwind. The more I moaned the more he massaged my pussy. "Cum for me." He said. I did.

Noel's dick was so hard when he slid inside of me. I moaned louder than usual. He held onto my hips with every thrust. It hurt but it felt so damn good at the same time. I wrapped my legs around him. He went deeper. "Oh, shit Noel." I said as he sped up. "It feels so good babe."

"I want you to come for me."

"I will. I will." I say in between moans. I came as Noel started to grind slowly.

When my orgasm ended Noel slid me further back into the bed. He turned me over onto my belly and took me from the back. He laid on top of me careful not to put all of his weight on my back. I whined my hips as he went in and out of my pussy. He grinded. He kissed my back and it sent lightning bolts through my body. "I'm cummin babe. I'm cummin." He sped up.

"Wet this dick up, this your dick." He whispers in my ear. "I'm about to cum with you."

Afterwards I got under the covers, Noel followed suit. Although it was warm in the house my naked body was cold. Noel pulled me closer to him, wrapped his arm around me and interlocked his fingers with mine. We just laid there in silence. Just the two of us. I liked it that way. It had been almost a month since the last time we've been anywhere alone outside of my bedroom. We barely had privacy at my house with my mom being there.

"Noel? Are we going to sell the condo or rent it out?"

"What do you want to do with it?"

"Keep it for the days you piss me off." I say with a light chuckle.

"If that's what you want to do then—" he says with a shrug.

I turn to look at him. "I love you Noel."

"I love you too."

"Thank you."

"For?"

"Always being there when I need you."

"Except for the one time you needed me most."

"You're not Superman babe, but really, every time I call you, you show up. You were coming that day too. That's enough for me. It makes me feel loved, special even."

"That's nothing out of the ordinary. I'm your man, I'm supposed to show up. I expect the same thing from you if we're together."

"Oh, we're together." I say as I flash my ring. "We're together real bad." I say with a wire filled smile.

"You're silly."

Chapter 27

I went over to Nathan's to meet him. He wanted me to ride with him to drop our parents off at the airport. Amora was going to ride back home with Kris and Ms. Ann. I was going to meet them back at the condo once Nathan and I got back from the airport.

When we arrived at the house Kris and Nathan were arguing about something. I grabbed Amora and walked her back to the living room with me. Their argument wasn't ours and I didn't want no parts in it. Nathan follows me to the living room. "Where you going Noel?"

"What exactly am I here for?" I ask with a chuckle. "One of ya'll could have just texted or called me."

"I wanted to talk with you about something after I dropped Mom and Dad off at the airport." Kris is now looking at Nathan then at me.

"You trying to talk to him about me?" she asks.

"Hell NO!" We don't talk about our women to each other. That's a problem a lot of couples have. Always talking to their family members about their significant others. Keep your business within your relationship." Nathan says.

"Wait, so if I need to vent who am I supposed to talk to?"

"Talk to God." Nathan and I both said in unison. We chuckle at ourselves repeating what our parents instilled in us.

"So ya'll don't vent to each other at all?" Kris asked.

Nathan said, "Don't get me wrong I love my brothers, but my relationship issues are mine and my significant other's problems. It's nothing to broadcast to the family or public. You gotta keep people out of your relationship."

"I agree but Amora's my sister. We vent to each other."

"That's normal for ya'll though. Ya'll are females. All women talk to each other." Nathan says.

Amora shakes her head. "It's some bitches you can't tell shit to. I only vent to a select few."

"So, babe, you don't vent to Angie and Mel?"

"I vent to Mel, yea." Amora says.

I ask. "But not Angie?"

"No. Angie can't fix any of my problems. Mel can. Kris can. They both give me nonbiased, sound advice. Angie, not so much."

"What about relationship advice?" Nathan asks Amara

"I'll go to Kris for that."

"Let me ask you this. If you and Noel were to fall out, do you think she'd still want him to come around?

"If I know my sister she'd probably get you to fix it."

"Yea, she'd probably do that because she knows you love him and that's my brother. What I'm saying is this, when couples involve a bunch of people in their relationship it never lasts. Our mom and dad raised us to keep our relationship out of the hands of other people no matter who it is. When you have so many mouths to your ear it's hard to hear who's saying what. You never want to give an outsider ammunition to use against your partner. That's like you putting out a hit to have your partner assassinated."

"Look at my man with the wisdom." Kris playfully nudges Nathan in his side.

"That's just real. It's levels to this relationship shit." Nathan says as he slaps Kris on her ass. "Now go make me a sandwich." We all laugh.

"You better stop showing off before you get your feelings hurt." She says still laughing.

"Amora how does it feel when you talk? Does it hurt?" Nathan asked.

"My throat is kinda scratchy. It hurts a little. My doctor told me to keep my conversations to a minimum though."

"I know you can't wait."

"Not at all. I'm going to pig out."

"We can have a dinner or something over here. I can get Norman to go all out if you want."

"Sounds nice but no thank you. Plus, he just went all out yesterday."

There's a knock at the door. "Speaking of the devil. That's Norman at the door." Nathan says as he gets up from the sofa to answer the door. In walks in all of our parents, Norman and Noble. We all greet each other.

****

The ride to the airport was a little emotional for my mom. She said that it had been a while since she was able to spend this much time with the four of us since we all moved to Dallas. Mom was always emotional. If I told her I had a bad day at work, she'd get emotional. Dad was in his own world during the ride. He finally cracked when we made it to the airport.

"Junior you're the oldest, I want you to keep these boys in check. I know you've calmed down a lot since you got with Kris. I'm proud of you for that. Noel, you do right by Amora. You done put a ring on her finger. You know what that means now don't you?"

"Yes Sir."

"I love you boys and I couldn't be prouder of the men you've become." Dad reaches out his hand for Nathan and I to shake.

"Everything your dad said." Mom says and hugs the both of us. "Ya'll are still my babies. I love all of you."

"We love you too, Mom." Nathan and I say in unison. We watch as our parents walk towards their boarding gate, then we head back to the car.

"So, what is it that you wanted to talk to me about? I got out of bed with my new fiancée for this talk. It better be worth it."

"I want to ask Kristine to marry me." Nathan says looking me square in the eyes.

I shrug. "So."

"NIGGA! I'm telling you I want to get married."

"I hear you. I just don't understand what the problem is."

"What the fuck is happening to me? I haven't even known her that long. That's some shit you'd do."

"So, you want me to tell you not to ask her?"

"No. Am I tripping though?"

"Bro I literally proposed to Amora yesterday in case you forgot. We haven't known each other a full three months yet. That doesn't mean that I'm less ready for marriage or not. I know you're ready because if you weren't we wouldn't be having this conversation right now."

"I know I love her. She does things for me that no woman has never done. When she's around I don't want her to leave. It's like I always want her around. She doesn't have to say a word and I'd still feel a sense of peace. She's the kind of woman every man dreams of having. I rush home to her after work. I call her all throughout the day. Want to know what's funny? When she decides to stay at her own place I can't sleep. It's like I need her with me. It's been nights where I'd pop up at her place at 2 and 3am because I couldn't sleep. I can't live without her."

"That's deep."

"You're telling me. Bro, I've never felt like this before in my life. If this is what being in love feels like—"

"That's exactly what it feels like. What makes it even better though is that it's okay to feel the way you do. Kris loves you Nate. We all can see that. We're just two brothers that got whipped by two sisters from the boot. They put that Voodoo on us." I said to lighten the mood. Nathan chuckled a little. "When you going to ask her?"

"I was thinking about doing something real nice for her for Valentine's day."

"Sounds like a plan. Let me know if there's anything you need me to do."

"You know I will. I don't have not one romantic bone in my body." Nathan says as he laughs at himself.

"You ain't never lying. I have to say it's shocking that Kris stayed around all this time."

Nathan shoots a look at me that let me know he didn't like my joke. "Noel she has a key to my crib bro. That speaks volumes. You know I always had hoes over but never gave anybody a key."

"Look at you growing up and becoming a man. You did well big bro. I'm proud of you too."

"You think I should tell Norman and Noble?"

"Shit we can go out tonight and drink to it if you want. Love like this is rare these days."

"I appreciate you Noel."

"I do what I'm supposed to do. You're my brother." We shook hands and went our separate ways.

Chapter 28

It was January 26th. I went in to have the wires completely removed and to get an x-ray on my ribs. However, I found out Noel and I were going to be parents. It was still very early; I was only six weeks. After doing all of my imaging my doctor cleared me to eat soft solids. She told me to ease into my normal diet gradually so I wouldn't have any complications with my jaw. My ribs were healing well. My next appointment was scheduled for the second week of February. It was an ultrasound appointment which was perfect because I was going to surprise Noel with the good news on Valentine's Day.

I reserved Noel and I the Byron Nelson Suite at The Las Colinas Resort soon as I left the doctor's office. It was a pretty penny, but my man was well worth it. I wanted to do something nice for my baby. Since I had been cleared, I wanted to show some gratitude. I had the reservation set up for us to have a private dining in our room. There were other luxuries like shopping and golfing but those were the least of my worries at the moment.

I needed to get something to wear for our dinner date. Noel was at work, so I was going to be alone for a couple of hours. I had to use my time wisely. I pulled out my laptop and began to browse the web. I searched for lingerie first because I wanted something cute and sexy. I knew that I'd have to find a dress to accommodate the lingerie also. I found a black lingerie set online. The set included a bra, a pair of panties, a garter belt, and lace thigh pieces. It was sexy. The panty was a thong with a sheer skirt with lace trimming. It all went together nicely.

Initially I wanted a red dress being it would be Valentine's Day. That idea went out of the window when I strolled across this black leather long sleeved dress by DF. It was a perfect complement to the lingerie I chose. I found a pair of metallic gold, stiletto leather sandals by Schutz, a gold pleated clutch by Loeffler Randall, and a pair of 14k yellow gold hoops by Nickho Rey that I could wear with the dress.

I had just clicked submit when my watch alerted me of the movement at my front door. It was Kristine coming to get an update on my doctor's visit. When I texted earlier, she was about to walk into a session. Her sessions usually ran anywhere from an hour to an hour and a half. As I was heading for the door she rang the bell again. "Okay! I'm coming." I yelled towards the door. Kris walked past me and headed straight for the fridge.

"I need a glass of wine."

"Long Day?" I asked.

"YES!"

"Well help yourself. Somebody needs to drink it."

While Kris was pouring herself a glass of wine she asked, "So what did the doctor say?"

"She told me that I was pregnant and to transition back to solid foods gradually." I laugh as Kris spits out her wine.

"Wait. What the fuck did you just say?" She looks at me with this big silly ass grin on her face.

"I'm pregnant." Kris screeched and ran in place.

"I'm going to be an auntie." She rubbed my belly. "I hope it's a girl so you can name her after me."

"Girl Please! One of you is enough." I responded with a chuckle.

"Have you told Noel yet?"

"No, I think I'll surprise him for Valentine's Day. I already reserved a room at The Las Colinas Resort."

"Ouu that's going to be nice Amora. Does Mom know?"

"Not yet. You know how she is. She's going to tell everybody and it's still too early."

"Yes, that is very true. She can't hold water." Kris said with a chuckle. "How far along are you?"

"Six weeks."

"Aww, my baby's having a baby." She said as she rubbed my belly again. I laughed at her.

"How was work?"

"Huh?"

"How was work?"

"Oh, girl who cares. I'm going to be an auntie. I can't wait."

"Look at this dress I just ordered to wear for Valentine's Day. Tell me what you think. I think it'll be cute to wear for dinner. I planned everything out." I told her as I was pulling up the site to show her the dress. "I was going to get a red dress but then I strolled across this one."

"I like that. It's nice. You have the body for it. Get you a pair of some bad ass stilettos and you'd be good to go."

"Already did. I told you; I've planned everything. My entire outfit is ordered and awaiting processing. I think I'm going to put my hair up in a bun." I say as I pick my hair up imitating a bun. "What you think."

"That'll be cute."

"What are you thinking about? You're being all dry now"

"You're planning for Noel, and I haven't put any thought into doing something for Nathan. You have me thinking now."

"You think ya'll are going to be together forever?"

"Yes. It's scary though. Mrs. Betty told me that a man would change for a woman he loved. I can't help but to wonder if he'd go back to the man he was before we got together. Running the streets and sleeping with different women. I'm just sitting back letting it all play itself out. So far so good. A girl popped up on us one day at the beginning of our relationship. I think it was the first time I stayed over. He flashed. He called her every cuss word in the dictionary. Later that night he gave me a key. He said that if any woman was going to pop up at his house, he rather it be me. He said that he had never given a key to a woman before because he knew he wasn't living right. Get this, he leaves his phone face up."

"That's it there. A cheating man is not about to let you see who's calling and texting him. That phone would be somewhere faced down and on vibrate."

"Right! I love him though Amora. I love him like you love Noel. That's what scares me. This feels too good to be true. He spoils me. He caters to every aspect of me. He's good to me. I don't want for anything. He wants me to move in with him, but my job is closer to my house."

"Sounds like you're in love Krissy Pooh. Have you asked him about moving into your house with you."

"I think I am in love."

"I'll be moving in with Noel soon. I'm going to lease the condo out for some extra income. Noel told me that I didn't have to get rid of it if I didn't want to, but I don't want to go into a marriage thinking something will happen, you know?"

"I hear you. I think I want to start a family with Nathan."

"For real?" I said with a little excitement in my voice.

"Not right now but in the future. He'd be an amazing father. Mr. Nathan taught them all how to be men if he didn't teach them anything else. That's another thing I love about Nathan. He's a real man. He's confident and baby confidence looks so good on a man. I mean look at him." We both laugh.

"One look at Noel and I mesmerized you hear me. I mean I couldn't feel my knees." I said as I laughed at the flashback in my mind.

"You're silly."

My watch notifies me that Noel's home. "Noel's here."

"Have you heard anything from the detectives recently?" Kristine asked me changing the subject.

"Not a word. It's a cold case at this point."

"That's that bullshit."

"They're out fighting and solving other crimes I guess."

"Hey babe." Noel says as he walked in. "What's up Kris?

"Hey Babe." I say back to Noel as he came over to kiss me.

"Hey Noel."

"What ya'll ladies in here talking about?"

"Kris is in love with Nathan." Kris looks at me with a 'what the fuck' expression on her face. "What? Ain't nothing wrong with being in love."

"Well it's Nathan. Noel says and laughs at his own joke. "He's a good dude. I think you've changed him for the better."

"I didn't change him, that was his own doing."

"Yea, we have a tendency to do that when we find a woman worth changing for." Kris and I shot each other a quick glance. Noel says as he winks at me.

"On that note, I'm about to head home to be with this so called changed man before he starts blowing me up." Kris kisses my cheek. "Call me if you need me. Let me know when your next appointment is so I can clear my schedule. I don't want to miss anything."

"Will do. Love you, Krissy Pooh."

"Love you too." Noel walks Kris to the door to make sure she makes it to her car safely.

Chapter 29

The day before my ultrasound appointment Detective Lee called me. He told me that the lab was able to retrieve a salvia sample from the envelope Noel had given him. He stated that the DNA traced back to Tia. The problem that he was he didn't have an updated address on her to bring her in for questioning. Her last known address was Noble's address as well.

Detective Lee told me that he already visited Noble to get him to confirm he didn't know the whereabouts of Tia. The only priors Tia had on her record was over fifteen years ago. She was charged with petty theft and served eighteen months in the Mesquite Juvenile Detention Center.

When Noel came home from work, I told him the news, but he said I was too late, Noble had already beat me to it. He went to the fridge to pour a glass of wine. "No thank you babe, I'm fasting from alcohol."

"Oh, I didn't know. You didn't tell me. Not that you had to, I'm just..." He was rambling.

"It's cool babe." I wrapped my arms around Noel's neck and kissed him. "I missed you today."

"I missed you too."

"How was work?"

"It was pretty laid back. We didn't have much to do at the office."

"Sounds like a fun day."

"I was thinking we could go out for dinner tonight."

"Can we go to The Capital Grille? We haven't been there yet."

Noel moves his hands to my ass and starts to caress it. "We can go wherever you want to go."

"It's a date then." I say with a big smile.

"It's a date."

"I'll start getting ready. Nothing fancy tonight though, it's too cold out there to be trying to be cute." I said to Noel. This weather certainly wasn't dress weather. New Orleans never got this cold in all of my life. I took a twenty-minute shower and got dressed. I put on a navy cashmere Ralph Lauren sweater, a pair of white Levi's skinny jeans, and a pair of navy Naturalizer boots that I bought from Dillard's. My hair was in a ponytail, so I decided to wear a pair of navy hoops. I grabbed my navy Kate Spade crossbody from my closet and headed back to the living room.

Noel walked in from the guest room looking all kinds of handsome. His scent had me in a choke hold. My man was sexy as hell. He had on his navy Ralph Lauren corduroy pants with a white dress shirt underneath his navy cashmere Ralph Lauren sweater. Noel completed his outfit with a tan Ralph Lauren belt and a pair of tan Cole Haan Oxfords. An intelligent, well-dressed man with confidence was a woman's dream come true.

"You want to be like me so badly. How did you know what I was going to wear?"

"I didn't. You said to dress down so." Noel shrugs. "Great minds think alike they say."

"Uh huh. I said with a sarcastic expression on my face.

"You ready?"

"I think so."

"Okay then, let's roll." Noel says as he lightly smacks my ass. After Noel sets the alarm, he walks to the passenger side to open the door for me. Then, he walks to the driver side and gets into the car.

"Can I ask you a question?" I asked Noel.

"Depends on what the question is."

"I'm serious Babe."

"What's up?"

"Do you think they'll find Jacob and Tia?"

"They better hope they find them before I do. You worried?"

"No."

Noel had a shocked expression on his face. He asked, "You're not?"

"Why should I be? Whatever's going to happen will happen."

"I guess that's true.

The rest of the ride Noel and I were silent. Noel listened to his ratchet music while I texted my girls. Kris was still trying to figure out what she wanted to do for Nathan on Valentine's Day. Mel was investigating some rich man that was accused of cheating on his wife with his stepsister. Angie was getting ready for work and Macey was about to get her back broke by some fine ass man she met at the gym. Macey was living her best life, and I wasn't mad at her.

When we made it to the restaurant Noel had the valet park the car, so I didn't have to walk too far. We walked into the restaurant hand in hand. The hostess greeted us and asked how many. Noel took the lead. "A table for two please. Can you give us something private, a little intimate?"

"Sure, you can follow me."

We followed her to a table towards the back of the restaurant. It was very intimate. I took the seat against the wall because I didn't like people walking behind me. I liked being aware of my surroundings at all times. More now than before. Noel slid his chair closer to me and wrapped his arm around me.

"You look sexy tonight."

"Thank you." I said as I blushed. "You look good too. I hope you're single. I might have to take you home with me."

"I'm sorry my love. I'm a happily engaged man." He said then winked.

I raise my left hand and wiggle my fingers. "Oh, is that right?" I say giggling like a teenager.

"That is absolutely right." Noel leans over to kiss me and my body tingled all over. I suddenly got hot. My panties were moist.

"Look, we came here to eat." I speak.

"Oh, I'm going to eat now and later." Noel said with a flirtatious expression on his face.

"My name is Amanda. I'll be your server this evening. Can I start you off with any drinks?"

"You can get me a glass of the Santa Margherita, Alto Adige, Pinot Grigio. What you want to drink Babe?" Noel asked me.

"The water is fine. Thank you."

"I'll bring it right over for you."

"Thanks." Noel said as the server walked away. "You want to order an appetizer?"

"I'm not sure yet." The server comes back with Noel's glass of wine. "Amanda, can you show me where the ladies' room is please?" I asked.

"Sure, follow me."

"I'll be right back Babe." I followed Amanda to the ladies' room. All of the different aromas were starting to get to me. I was getting nauseous. I wanted my pregnancy to be a surprise to Noel, but I didn't know if I could hide it too much longer with the morning sickness kicking in. I had to make up a lie and quickly. I splashed my face with water hoping that it would help a little. I dried it with a paper towel then, I headed back to the table.

"Took you long enough. I was about to come look for you. Everything okay?"

I gave him a fake smile. "Yes Babe. Everything's fine."

Amanda came back to the table. "Would you like to order any starters?"

"No thank you. We're going to go straight to our entrees."

"Okay, what can I get for you?"

"I'll like the 10oz filet mignon cooked medium well with a side of sautéed spinach please."

"Sure, and for you beautiful?"

I blushed a little. "I'll like to try the seared citrus glazed salmon with sautéed spinach as well.

"The lamb chops are served with a white wine of your choice. Would you like another glass of wine sir?" She said looking at Noel.

"No, thank you. My water is fine." Noel said.

"Okay. I have an order for a 10 oz filet mignon medium well with a side of sautéed spinach and an order seared citrus glazed salmon with a side of sautéed spinach as well. No wine."

"Correct." I speak.

"I'll get this to the kitchen for you. Is there anything you need at the moment that I can get for you?

"Yes. Can I get a glass of Sprite please?"

"Absolutely. I'll be right back with that Sprite. Amanda leaves to get my drink.

"Amora what's wrong with you? It's something you're not telling me. Something is up. What is it?"

"Nothing Noel. Everything is fine." I lied. I was feeling worst the longer I sat in the restaurant. I needed something to settle my stomach.

"Look at me." Noel grabs my chin with his hand and I turn my head away. "See. You're lying to me. That's the only time you don't look at me. Babe what's wrong? You were fine a few minutes ago."

"I'm nauseous Noel. I know you wanted this date, but the different aromas are making me sick."

"I'll have her make the food to go then."

"You don't have to do that. I'll drink my Sprite and I'll be fine.

Amanda walks over with my Sprite. "Amanda, my fiancé isn't feeling well. Can you have them make our food to go please? Noel asked.

"Certainly. I'll bring your check. I hope you feel better."

"Thank you." I say with a shy smile.

Amanda walks away again heading to the kitchen. Noel continued to play Inspector Gadget. It took over 30 minutes for Amanda to bring our food. I wish she hadn't because soon as she sat the food on the table I had to speed walk to the ladies' room. Noel was on my heels. I couldn't speak. I was trying hard not to vomit before making it to the toilet. My surprise wasn't going as planned. Once I made it to the toilet, I let it all out. It hurt my ribs a little bit.

"Amora what's wrong? What can I do?" I heard Noel ask me. He was in the ladies' room with me. Noel gave zero fucks that it was the ladies' room. He for damn sure didn't care that other ladies were in there as well. "Can one of you ladies be kind enough to get the valet to bring our car around? I want to get her out of here as quickly as possible."

"I can do it for you young man." I heard an older woman say to him.

"Thank you so much. Here's my ticket and cash for the tip. Thank you so much." I heard the door open and close again. Noel started to rub my back. "Babe what can I do?"

When it felt like I had nothing else left in my stomach to vomit I walked over to the sink and rinsed my mouth out. Noel

241

was still in the ladies' room looking lost. "We can go now." I said as I dried my hands and face.

"You going to tell me what's wrong with you?"

"Must've been something I ate earlier. The smells were just too much.

Chapter 30

Amora spent the entire duration of our ride home in her phone. I'd never seen her sick like she was tonight. I didn't know what to think. I made a mental note to pay more attention to her once we got home. I asked her if she was feeling better. She said that she was feeling much better, but I still thought she was lying to me. She was fine before we left home. She was fine up until she wasn't.

The food was still hot when we made it home. Amora went straight to the bathroom to rinse her mouth out while I took our plates out of the bag. She joined me in the living room when she was done. I was sitting on the couch getting ready to untie my shoes when she walked up to me.

"I do have something to talk with you about. I really wanted to wait and surprise you, but my plan doesn't seem to be going as planned."

"What's up?" I asked with a stern look on my face. I wanted her to know that I was serious."

She sits down next to me. "It's not the easiest thing to tell you but it's —"

"What is it, Amora?" I raised my voice a little.

"Calm down Noel, sheesh."

"I am calm. What is it?" I sat back on the couch looking at Amora's blank face. Whatever it was, was getting the best of her. I could tell. I'd never seen her as nervous as she was before.

"I love you Noel."

"I know this. I love you too. Move on with it." I said as I moved my hand in a circular motion.

Amora smiles one of the biggest most beautiful smiles I'd ever seen planted on her face. "Babe, I'm pregnant."

"You're fucking with me?" I say with a nervous chuckle.

She shakes her head. "No, I'm not. I planned on surprising you with the news on Valentine's Day, but the morning sickness started to kick in."

I stood up and grabbed her off of the couch. I hugged her tightly and kissed her. "I love you so much Amora. You have no idea."

"I kinda do." She said looking into my eyes as she started to kiss me again.

"How far along are you?"

"Two months." She tells me.

I hugged Amora and I caressed her ass. I pulled her sweater and under shirt over her head exposing her soon to be milk filled breast. I pulled my sweater over my head and Amora started unbuttoning my dress shirt. I unhooked my belt and unbuttoned my pants. I kicked my shoes off. Amora took her pants off leaving only her underwear on. She pushed me back onto the coach. I used my feet to remove my pants completely.

Amora pulled my boxers down freeing my already erect dick. She then began to kiss the head, it jumped. She took the head into her mouth. I threw my head back onto the couch. "Fuck." I watched as she bobbed up and down sucking my dick. I slid her ponytail holder out of her hair allowing her long, silky hair to fall free. We made eye contact. "Oh shit. That's it. Suck it just like that."

She wrapped her hand around my dick and masturbated my shaft as she licked and sucked my balls. I moaned. Amora had never given me head before. I never intended to ask her to give me head. To be honest I didn't think she knew how to give a blow job. This was a hell of a surprise. Amora took her panties off, straddled me and eased down on my dick. "Fuck."

"You like that?" Amora asks me.

"Hell yea, I like it." Amora rode my dick so effortlessly. I sucked on her breast. I licked and sucked her neck. She grinded so hard. My dick was deep in her swollen pussy and she was taking it.

"I love you Noel." She says as she whined her hips. Her pussy was so wet and warm. I lost it. She started to ride more aggressively; I knew that meant she was about to cum. I grabbed her neck and made her kiss me. She let out a loud moan and just like that we were done. I slapped her ass.

I laid back on the couch and pulled Amora to my chest. We needed a break after all of the work we'd just put in. She ended up falling asleep in that position. I listened to the rhythm of her breathing. Her body felt warm up against mine. I started to think about what she told me. I was going to be a father then a thought crossed my mind. I woke Amora up, "Babe you need to eat something."

"I'm not hungry Babe" she said with a raspy voice.

"The baby might be hungry. You puked everything up Amora."

"Noel!" She said sounding aggravated. "I'm going in my room. Do not wake me up again please."

I took my phone out of my pants pocket and texted my brothers through our group chat.

Me: Ya'll still up?

Nate: Yea I'm up, what's up?

Norman: Yea I'm up.

Noble: What's up?

Me: Amora's pregnant. She's been puking all night. I tried to get her to eat and she

caught an attitude with me.

Norman: I'm trying to make sure I read this right.

Noble: Norman shut up. Just say you can't read. LOL

Nate: It's the hormones. Her body has to adjust to accommodate the new person it's developing.

Norman: So, you're telling us that we're going to be uncles? You didn't tell us that ya'll were trying.

Me: Nigga, I don't have to tell you what I'm doing in the bedroom. LMAO. Tf wrong with this nigga.

Noble: That's your brother.

Nate: I keep telling ya'll niggas that Norman was adopted. When ya'll gonna start listening to me? LOL

Me: Is there something I can do to help her?

Nate: Nope, you just have to let it run its course. You better hope she doesn't get mean. I think Kris gonna be grouchy when she gets pregnant. She's already mean. LOL. Don't tell her I told ya'll that.

Me: Secret's safe with me.

Noble: How many months is she?

Me: Two. She said.

Norman: *How you feeling about all of this?*

Me: *Excited. I've been waiting for this for a long time.*

Nate: *I'll get with ya'll at the office tomorrow. We gotta celebrate.*

Noble: *Definitely.*

Norman: *Ight*

Me: *That's a bet.*

I closed our food up and put it all in the fridge thinking maybe Amora would go back to it later. I took a shower and got in bed with my fiancé. I wrapped my arm around her and pulled her closer to me. She squirmed a little to get comfortable then to sleep we both went.

Chapter 31

I woke up Valentine's Day morning just as excited as I could be. It was nice and toasty in the house. Noel must've woken up early because the smell of pancakes and turkey bacon was seeping through the vent in my bedroom. I was getting ready to slide out of bed when Noel walked in carrying breakfast on a bed tray. The aroma was so heavenly, my stomach started rumbling.

He had the tray set up so nicely. There was a single pink rose alongside a small plate of turkey bacon and eggs. On another plate was a stack of three fluffy medium sized pancakes. There was also a small bowl of fruit with a glass of orange juice to wash it all down. I noticed a small square box with PANDORA written on it in the corner of the table. I picked it up once Noel sat the table down across my lap.

"Good morning beautiful." He says as he kisses me.

"Good morning handsome." I said while wrapping my arms around Noel's neck and kissing him. "Where's your plate?"

"I'll have to eat on the run. I want to get my work done early so I can leave the office early. Enjoy your breakfast. Right now, I want you to eat and have an amazing day at work." Noel said as he caressed my cheek then kissed me again.

"Thank you so much babe. My day is already amazing."

"Oh really? Why is that?"

"Because I have you."

"Don't start nothing we can't finish. I have to get to work babe."

"I'll save it for our date later." I said, giving Noel a flirtatious look. "I love you."

"I love too Amora."

I opened the PANDORA box as Noel was walking out of the bedroom. Inside of the box was a charm bracelet. "This is soooo cute." I said out loud as I removed the bracelet from the box. The bracelet itself was silver with a mixture of silver and rose gold charms. The first dangle charm was a pair of baby shoes and a bottle. The next was a padlock and key dangle charm. In between each dangle charm was a small heart charm. The last dangle charm spelled out the word family. Noel's gift of choice was astounding. It left me both speechless and emotional.

After gathering myself, I dried my tears and began to eat my breakfast. My food was everything. The bacon was cooked to perfection. My pancakes were crispy around the edges just the way I liked them. My eggs were scrambled with finesse. The orange juice was freshly squeezed, and the fruit were also fresh. My man had stepped it up big time for our first Valentine's Day.

"Alexa play 90s R&B." I said as I climbed out of bed to start getting ready for work. I laid out my marine-colored Veronica Beard suit across my bed along with my red Courrèges ribbed blouse. I wanted to incorporate a little red for the occasion. I complemented my suit with a pair of red, Suede ankle-strap sandals by Stuart Weitzman.

Once I got what I wanted to wear out of the way I walked into the kitchen to put the dirty dishes in the sink. To my surprise there were more gifts waiting for me in the living room. There were "I love you" balloons, giant bouquets of assorted roses, lilies and an assortment of gift bags. I couldn't help but get emotional. I called Noel. "This is Noel." He said as he answered.

"Thank you so much babe. I love all of it." I said. crying into the phone. "I love you so much Noel. I want to hug and kiss you babe. Why did you do this and leave me like this? Babe this is so beautiful." I say as I'm sniffling.

"I'm happy you like your gifts. I tried to find something as beautiful as you, but I was unsuccessful."

"Noel you are amazing. I am in awe. You've really outdone yourself."

"It's our first Valentine's together, I had to make it a memorable one."

"This is definitely one for the books." I said as I started walking around the living room smelling the flowers.

"Where are you now?"

"I'm still at home, why?"

"I was just asking. What time are you heading to your office?"

"In a little bit. I still have to shower and get dressed."

"Ok, well let me know how your ride to work was once you make it. Love you babe." He said before disconnecting the call.

I went on to take my shower and get dressed. After getting dressed I brushed my hair up in a high ponytail and gave myself another once over. I wasn't anxious about going into the office, but I needed to have a quick pow wow with Jake. He'd been letting me work from home a few days a week to give my ribs time to completely heal. I'd gotten spoiled with working from home. I still did site visits every now and then when needed. On my way out, I stopped to read one of the cards from one of the bouquets. It read:

> Before I met you, I knew you.
> Before I held you, I felt you.
> Before I saw you, I knew exactly what you should look like, only to not recognize you upon first sight.
> You are both everything and nothing I expected, all included in one beautiful package.
> You are Love, personified.
> Do me the honor of being Love's Valentine?
> Noel

"Oh my God, what did I do to deserve this man?" I asked myself aloud. I held the card to my heart and meditated on the words a bit before walking out of the house. "What in the —?" I say while locking the door to my condo. There was a black Audi SQ5, wearing a bow, parked in my parking space.

"This is why his ass asked me where I was." I say thinking out loud. I started to call Noel but remembered he told me to let him know how my drive was once I made it to work. Noel was spoiling me, and I loved every minute of it.

The Audi was fully loaded. It had everything from black leather seats with diamond stitching to heated and cooled cupholders. I only noticed that because I found the keys sitting in the cupholder. *"My baby got me a sunroof."* I thought to myself. I loved having a sunroof for the days I wanted to let my hair blow in the wind. I was adjusting the mirrors when I noticed a black car creeping by in the rearview. I figured it was one of Mel's guys, so I didn't over analyze the situation. I was entirely too busy smiling from ear to ear.

During the ride to work I was sitting on top of the world. I had my music playing in the background while I got lost in my thoughts. The memories of my ultrasound appointment crossed my mind. Kris was with me at the appointment. I ended up being a late for my appointment because I had to vomit every five minutes. The toothpaste made me sick. My tea made me sick. Everything made me sick. Morning sickness was making me sick. I ended up having to call Noel on FaceTime, he had a business meeting the same morning of the appointment that couldn't be rescheduled. While the sonographer was completing my transvaginal ultrasound, she showed us the baby's heartbeat and printed out a few images for me to take as a keepsake. Kris and I both cried while watching my little one on the monitor.

My parking space was empty when I pulled into the parking garage. I parked my new baby and headed into the building. I texted Noel as I walked into the elevator. He responded rather quickly.

Husband: You have good timing. My meeting just ended.

Me: The ride was phenomenal.

Me: BTW thank you for my new ride.

Husband: My pleasure.

Me: What's the reason?

Husband: We have a baby coming. You needed something bigger.

Me: That is true. Once I finish up here, I'm going back home, I'm not staying the whole day.

Husband: Cool. Let me know when you leave the office. I'll come to join you.

Me: K. I love you.

Husband: Love you too.

Erica was sitting at her desk when I approached her "Good morning, Erica." She looked up from behind her computer with her eyebrow raised. I smiled and walked directly to my office. I talked to Erica enough to know why she looked at me the way that she did. I hadn't made her aware that I was stopping by the office.

"Good morning Ms. Scott. I didn't know you were coming in today. It's not like you to not give me a heads up." Erica said as she followed me to my office. "Why are you even here?" She said with a sarcastic tone. "It's Valentine's Day. It's a day of love. It's your day."

I waved my hand towards the roses. "Well, I'm happy I did show up because Noel would've been disappointed had I not."

"Please! Noel worships the ground you walk on. He would've been just fine."

"You're probably right. He's showered me with so many gifts this morning already." I turned to smell a bouquet of roses.

"Amora, can I ask you a question?"

"You called me by my first name so this can't be work related." I said with a you've got my attention expression on my face.

"No but it's Amora related. Are you gaining weight or is that a baby bump I see?"

I unconsciously rub my belly. "Shh. Yes, we are expecting. I don't want to tell everyone yet. I'm waiting until we're out of the danger zone."

"I'm so excited. I hope it's a little Amora." Erica said with excitement.

"Noel and I both want a girl as well. I'm still processing it all right now. It really came as a surprise. All of it really—"

"Well, your meeting with Jake is scheduled in," she looks at her watch, "ten minutes actually." Ironically enough I was actually at the office to meet with Jake. "I've returned most of your messages like you asked me to. I've made files for our three new contacts. There's a prospective contractor in the works as well. He wanted to speak with you about a broken water line or something like that."

I was trying to figure out what made Erica switch the topic so quickly then I got my answer. Stephanie walked past my office. "Do you have the contact information for the contractor? Thanks for the subject change."

"Absolutely. I do have that information for you though. Let me get it from my desk." After Erica handed the post-it to me, I headed to Jake's office to meet with him.

Jake's door was slightly open when I approached his office, but I knocked anyway. "Good morning, Jake," I say as I walk in. Jake was just as excited to see me as Erica. It was like I hadn't been back at work since the assault happened. It made me feel special to have everyone greet me with smiles.

"Amora! Good morning. How are you?" Jake said as he walked from behind his desk to pull out a chair for me. "I thought you'd changed your mind once 9:30 rolled around. I know you usually like to get started early."

"I do. I do. This morning was a little emotional for me. My fiancée surprised me with many gifts, so I spent most of the morning crying like a baby. Happy tears of course." I said with a chuckle.

"Trust me, I know that feeling oh so well. I did the same thing for my wife before coming into the office. I'll be leaving after our meeting to set up another surprise I have planned for her."

"You don't find too many guys excited about Valentine's Day."

"Well, that's true but today is also our anniversary. We've been married twelve years today."

"Congratulations. That's beautiful."

"Thank you. Have you guys set a date yet?"

"No, not yet. I was thinking about next year some time."

"Let me tell you this, DO NOT let family nor friends pressure you to get married in their time. Make those plans with your spouse ALONE."

"Duly noted."

"Okay now that the adult stuff is out of the way let's get this meeting started shall we." Jake says with a chuckle. Erica hinted something about a prospective client."

"Yes, she gave me the contractor's contact info." I say as I hand the post-it to Jake.

"Great! I will reach out to set up a meeting." Jake always got right down to business leaving no stone unturned. We were able to get all of our notes and reports completed in less than two hours. Afterwards, we were free to leave and enjoy the rest of our day with the loves of our lives.

I called Noel to let him know that I was on my way home. He told me that his client pushed their meeting to a later time and that he wouldn't be home until check in time at the hotel. It worked out because there were a few things that I needed to pack before checking into the hotel.

I ordered Noel a customized Whiskey bar set and a pair of Gucci cuff links that I wanted to pack. It wasn't a new car, but it was something I knew my man would love. I was going to give him what he needed after our private dinner if you know what I mean.

Chapter 32

When I finally made it home, I couldn't take my shoes off quickly enough. "That feels so much better." I say aloud. I sat on the couch and went through a couple of gift bags Noel left on the coffee table. One of the bags had a bottle of my favorite perfume. In another was a framed copy of our ultrasound. I immediately cried a river. It was the most beautiful gift I'd ever received. "Daddy blew your picture up for everyone to see." I say as I rub my belly.

Since Noel was going to be a while, I decided to burn time by taking a hot bubble bath. I carried our baby's picture with me to my bedroom and placed it on the nightstand closest to my side of the bed. Then, I started my bath water. I added a couple drops of rose scented oil and a little Dr. Teal's foaming bath to the water. I wanted to relax a little before our evening shenanigans. I told Alexa to play my sexy playlist and raised the volume. Once the water reached my desired level, I got in.

The water was the perfect temperature. The scent of my rose oil filled the bathroom. This was exactly what I needed, this moment. My healing was progressing, I was going to be back in the office soon and Jake was going to be assigning more site visits to me. Noel and I had a wedding to plan and a baby to prepare for. This soak was just what I needed to pause my thoughts. I drifted off to sleep.

"Bath time is over bitch," is what snapped me out of my moment of relaxation. Curtis. Jacob. Whoever the hell he wanted to be was standing next to the bathtub with a gun pointing at me. "Don't scream or I will shoot you. I didn't come here to hurt you." He says as he hands me my robe.

As I stood up to get out of the bathtub, Jacob turned his back to me. I put my robe on and tied it tight. For some strange reason I believed that he wouldn't hurt me. I assumed that if he wanted to it would've been done already. "How did you get in here?"

"Are you done?" He asks.

"Yes." Jacobs turns around to help me out of the bathtub, never lowering the gun from my head.

"Listen, I'm here to warn you about Tia. First, I want to apologize to you for what I did to you. I'm so sorry Amora. I wanted to hate you so badly but after following you and watching you interact with other people, I realized that you were just doing your job.

"Yes, I was." I say as tears start to fall from my eyes. "It was my first day on the job and I wanted to be taken seriously. I admit that I could've handled the situation differently."

Jacob held my arm and guided me to the living room. "I came here because Tia is coming. She snapped when we saw you leaving the doctor's office Tuesday." He signaled for me to sit on the couch. "I'm going to show Tia just how much I love her."

The door opened and my eyes grew wide thinking that it could've been Noel. Jacob pointed his gun towards the door. I yelled Jacob's name as loud as I could to warn Noel. Only it wasn't Noel.

"Why the fuck are you here Jacob?"

"I needed to talk to you to stop you from killing Amora."

"To stop me from killing Amora?" Tia repeats as she closes the door and locks it. "What? You love this bitch? You don't even know her."

"No, I don't love her, I love you, Tia. I've always loved you. I've been in love with you since our foster parents took you in but to you, I've never been good enough. I did everything you've ever asked of me. I'd do anything for you. I'm here now trying to protect you. You think the nigga you're doing all of this shit for loves you? Look around Tia. You're in the house he shares with the woman HE loves. He does not love you, Tia."

"He does love me but this bougie bitch is in the way." Tia says as she grabs me from the couch.

"What do you want from me Tia? Why are you here?" I asked her as I searched her with my eyes. She didn't have a weapon, not one that I could see anyway. Jacob had a gun, but I wasn't sure whose side he was really on. I was indefensible and there wasn't anyone that could save me.

"I want Noel. Where is he?"

"He's at the office with Noble. You do remember him, right? He's the brother that actually loves you." Tia slaps me.

"Shut the fuck up, nobody asked you anything." She turns to Jacob. "Can you believe the excitement I felt when you told me you knew her bougie ass? When you told me that she was the reason you got fired I was ecstatic. I put my plan in motion. You were supposed to get her to fall for you and once she did, I was going to have Noel for myself. The better-looking brother. The brother that's more financially stable. He's the better option." She says shooting a look at me. "But NO, you had to fuck it all up. I told you to beat her to death. You brought the bitch to the ER. Noel acts like she's a fucking gift from God. He waits on her bougie ass hand and foot.

"And Mrs. Betty. Don't get me started on that old shit nosed bitched. She was kissing Amora's ass from the minute she met her. That bitch never liked me. This bitch must have diamonds in her pussy or something." Tia says as she points her finger in my face. "You doing voodoo on people? Yea, you're one of those voodoo witch bitches."

"Tia STOP IT!" Jacob yells.

"Fuck you, Jacob. You fucked this up for me. YOU! Now I have to fix it. I always have to fix your fuck ups. You had one job. ONE!" Jacob raised his gun and aimed it at Tia. "You're going to shoot me? Let me ask you a question. How is she still breathing right now?"

"I couldn't leave her for dead Tia. She's innocent."

"Of course, you couldn't because you're weak. You've always been weak.

"Who was there when you didn't have shit? ME! Who robbed people to feed you Tia? ME! Who found your mom's husband and killed him for molesting you? ME! I did that for you because I LOVE YOU. Make that the last muthafucking time you call me weak." Jake says to Tia.

I watch as tears are rolling down Tia's face. In the blink of an eye Tia's pulls a gun from behind her back and aims it at me. BANG!

Tia looks Jacob square in the eyes. "Could you have done that Jacob? No, you couldn't." She says as she shakes her head. "Why? Because you're weak. You'll never be Noel. I will never love you. You good for nothing pussy."

BANG...

BANG.

****

Meanwhile, the sound of sirens pierced the air. When I arrived at Amora's condo it was surrounded by cops. I heard one of Mel's guys tell an officer that two people, a female and male entered Amora's condo. He even showed photos of the both of them. We all stood outside hoping for the best then there was a shot.

I watched as the S.W.A.T team put on their vests and shields, then there was another shot. Less than a minute later there was another shot. My knees got weak. My heart started to race. The officers started accessing the condo. The front door was unlocked. I started to silently pray that Amora was okay. I wasn't ready to lose her, not like this. I sent a message to my brothers in our group chat.

The coroner's van pulled up few minutes later and I almost lost it. I watched as a set of EMTs ran into the condo. I called Kris, she said she was already on the way. I was sick. My stomach was doing flips. I needed Amora and the baby to be okay.

"So far we have two DOAs." I overheard an officer say to a fellow officer.

"It's three people in there. How's the third person?"

"I'm sorry Sir. Who are you?"

"That's my fiancée's place. She was working from home."

"Follow me Sir, you may be able to help us." I followed the cop to the entrance of Amora's condo. He stopped to give me a pair of protective booties and gloves. "You need to put these on over your shoes and put these gloves on to avoid evidence being destroyed.

"Yes Sir." I said assuring the officer that I understood completely.

"Okay, we'll head in."

I followed closely behind the officer. We walked through the living room. There were two bodies covered with white sheets. I felt sick to my stomach. I wanted to vomit. The officer leads me to Amora's bedroom. The medics had my baby lying on a stretcher. I watched as they did CPR to resituate her. "Amora." I couldn't help but yell out.

"WE HAVE A PULSE! We have a pulse. Let's get her to the ambulance now!" They picked the stretcher up and strapped it to the bed. "Make room. Clear the way. We have one live female heading your way. She's been shot, through and through." The Medic said as she radioed to the hospital.

"Is Amora the resident of the condo?" The officer asked me.

"Yes, she is."

"Thank you. You may want to catch up to that ambulance. I got what I needed."

I took off running behind the medics. I had to be with my baby. By the time I made it to the sidewalk the ambulance was pulling off. I jumped into my car and followed them. My phone rang, it was Nathan. I answered through my Bluetooth. "What's up?"

"I just wanted you to know it's me following you."

"Okay."

"How is she?"

"She's breathing. That's all I know right now."

"Do you know what happened?"

"It looked like a scene from the story of "*Romeo and Juliet.* The guy and Tia were both dead. "

"Tia, Tia."

"Yep."

"FUCK!"

"Nate!"

"I gotta catch Noble before he gets there. I'll take care of Noble. You just worry about Amora and keep us posted. I'll be there in a minute."

The Epilogue

One Year Later

Our baby girl was born on September 1st. Noel thought Bella would fit and I agreed. She was so beautiful, hence the name. Our baby girl was born weighing 6 lbs. and 10 oz. She was a little over 19 inches long. Thankfully, I didn't have any complications during my pregnancy nor labor. Our baby girl was healthy.

I'd finally moved in with Noel, but I kept my condo. I decided to rent it out for an extra income. Noel paid to have it deep cleaned after the debacle with Tia and Jacob. It looked brand new when they were finished with it.

Noel and Nathan turned one of the guestrooms into a nursery. Kris and I did most of the decorating. I hung up Bella's ultrasound picture on the wall across from her crib along with pictures of Noel and me. I wanted her to be able to see us even

Dree Coleman

when we weren't physically in the room. Bella's nursery was picture perfect.

I became Mrs. Noel Brown on December 14th, Noel's birthday. We had a small wedding party consisting of our immediate families and our closest friends. We didn't have a traditional wedding; however, our wedding was definitely one we'd never forget. We danced the night away. It was one of the best nights of my life and yet we had forever to go.

As I sat in my glider rocking Bella, I could hear the fellas arguing about the Superbowl. I pick up my phone to text Noel about the noise when there's a knock at the door. "Come in." I try to say quiet enough not to wake Bella. The door slowly opens and to my surprise it's Mr. Nathan.

He tiptoes in as he whispers, "You have a minute to chat with your old man?"

"I sure do." I say with a smile.

"I won't hold you too long, but I wanted to talk with you about your new life." He says as he takes a seat in the recliner next to the window. Noel usually sits in it when he's rocking Bella to sleep. "I know today is probably a hard day for you considering your circumstances but don't give it the power to bring you down. Betty and I came out here to take over Bella so that you and Noel could make a more pleasant memory today. I know that you will never forget about what has happened to you. None of us will forget that day but you're the one that lived it. You live that day everyday. I know you do. You are blessed, baby girl. Do not allow that one day to hold your mind prisoner. So, you go ahead and put Bella in her crib to finish her nap. Take yourself a nice hot bubble bath and get dressed. Betty has already made dinner reservations for the two of you. We will take good care of Bella. This is your time enjoy every bit of it that you can." Mr. Nathan says to me before leaving the nursery.

I laid Bella in crib and headed to my bedroom. Noel was already in there when I walked in. "I'm about to take a bath, care to join me?"

"What kind of question is that." Noel says as he wraps his arms around my waist, and I wrap my arms around his neck. "I'll go wherever you go."

"I love you babe."

The End